Wild Pony Island

Wild Pony Island

STEPHEN W. MEADER

Illustrated by Charles Beck

SOUTHERN SKIES
LITTLE ROCK, ARKANSAS
www.southernskies.com

Foreword

When people "discover" Ocracoke, they inevitably become excited. The island and the village have a strange, unspoiled quality that is unique.

In the first place, the very difficulty of reaching Ocracoke makes a visit an adventure. It is the most remote of the Outer Banks islands—a narrow strip of sand some sixteen miles long, separated from the North Carolina mainland by the broad waters of Pamlico Sound. Its four-hundred-odd inhabitants are sturdy, self-reliant, God-fearing people, most of them descended from families that have lived there for two centuries. Fishing and shrimping provide their principal livelihood.

Because local opportunities are so limited, many of the young men go off to sea or to mainland cities. Mention Ocracoke in almost any gathering around Baltimore or Philadelphia, and you are likely to find a harbor pilot or the skipper of a tugboat or tanker coming up to shake your hand. He'll tell you with a shy smile that he grew up on Ocracoke and plans to go back there when he retires.

The famous Banker ponies have been on the island at least as long as the people. Now that a fenced range is provided for them, you'll no longer see ponies wandering through the village. But they are still there, and Ocracoke boys still have the fun of riding them.

In this story I have tried to use the form of speech that is heard among people who have never left the island. It has a quaint charm that seems to have been handed down from colonial days. I have also given my fictional characters the old family names so common in Ocracoke. A few of them—Captain Howard and Chief Ben O'Neal, for example—are the names of real people. And anyone who knows the place will have no difficulty in recognizing "Mr. and Mrs. Randall."

I am indebted to a number of people for this book. In particular, I would like to express my gratitude to an old friend, Paul C. Smith, who first interested me in Ocracoke; to Carl Goerch, whose fine book about the island whetted my appetite; to David Stick, for facts obtained from "Graveyard of the Atlantic" and "The Outer Banks of North Carolina"; and finally to Theodore and Alice Rondthaler, without whose understanding help the writing would have been impossible.

1959   STEPHEN W. MEADER

Wild Pony Island

Chapter One

On his fourteenth birthday Rick Landon woke up at six in the morning and saw a pale streak of sunshine coming in the room's one window. It was a small, rather dirty window, and it looked out over gray tenement roofs toward a corner of Prospect Park. A few treetops were visible over there, but if they had birds in them, they were too far away for any songs to be heard.

Rick got out of bed carefully, so as not to disturb his younger brother Joey. He scowled and yawned as he looked through the window. Below was a tiny back yard, bare except for two or three trash cans and a network of clotheslines. There was no grass, but a small clump of weeds grew raggedly in one corner. An alley cat prowled along the fence top. There was certainly nothing in that part of Brooklyn to tell that spring had come, but because Rick had known no other place since he was six, he didn't miss the grass or flowers. All he thought at the moment was that this wouldn't be much of a birthday.

For months he had known just what he would like for a present. It was a television set. Not a big one or a new one. He would have settled for a second-hand receiver with a ten-inch screen, just so it would let him watch his favorite Westerns. When he hinted about it to his mother, she had merely pursed her lips and said, "Well, some day, maybe. We'll see."

Rick knew they didn't have much money. Mrs. Landon pieced out her widow's pension by working as a clerk at a neighborhood delicatessen store half of each day. Even so she was hard put to feed and clothe the three of them, and the rent of their fourth-floor walk-up flat was high.

If his father had lived, the boy thought bitterly, things might have been different. But Richard Landon, Chief Petty Officer in the Coast Guard, had been killed eight years ago. People said then that he had died a hero's death. Now everybody seemed to have forgotten—everybody except Rick's mother, anyway. She still kept the faded front page of a newspaper that showed his picture and told how he had been struck on the head by a falling derrick boom while trying to rescue a man from the deck of a freighter that was afire.

Rick remembered him dimly as a big, smiling man who used to take him to Ebbets Field to watch the old Brooklyn Dodgers play ball. In those days they had lived in a nice little house out beyond Jackson Heights. It had a yard big enough for a few flowers and the baby's pen. But after the funeral things changed. The pension wasn't enough to keep up payments on the house, and Mrs. Landon had moved her small family into the city, where she could find some work to help out.

The boy had hated Brooklyn at first. Now he had become used to it—the jarring rumble of traffic; the smell of cooking cabbage in the apartment below; the grumpy people who jostled and scolded on the sidewalks. Of course there was some fun, too. A few blocks away there was a play street, where you could always find a game of stickball. If you had a few coins, you could see a movie or go to the ice-cream parlor, down on the corner. There was a jukebox

12

there, and some of the older kids hung around the place most of the time.

P.S. 68, where Rick went to school, was a grimy three-story brick building, more than fifty years old. He hated school. He hated the dark stairs and corridors, the dingy classrooms, and the smell of disinfectant. Usually he hated the teachers. They were too busy trying to keep some kind of order in the overcrowded rooms to put much effort into making learning seem interesting.

This was one of the "tough" districts, and most of the teachers were men. Women were nervous and sometimes got panicky when they found themselves facing overgrown youths like Mike Selensky and Big Jake Suchek and Tough Tony Lambretta. Those three had a special treatment for lady teachers. They slouched in their seats and grinned and stared, never answering a question. When they did open their mouths, it was to guffaw loudly at some other pupil's reply.

But there was one young woman who stood up to them undaunted. She was dark and intelligent-looking and her name was Miss Vronsky. She took the insolent stares without fidgeting. By sheer force of will she made them listen to her quiet voice and even succeeded in getting them to recite when called on.

"She's no square," Tony Lambretta admitted. "Miss Vronsky's got a lot o' guts. If I could read good, she could even maybe make me like English!"

When he was smaller, Rick had read a great deal. His mother had found books for him at the public library. Now he had decided that was kid stuff, and when he read at all, it was comics or paperback Westerns. If he had his choice of a career when he grew up, he was pretty sure he would be a cowboy.

By the time he had put on his clothes, he could hear his

mother getting breakfast. He gave young Joey a shake to wake him up, washed in the tiny bathroom, and went into the kitchen.

"Happy birthday, Ricky!" His mother greeted him with a smile.

She was a thin little woman with a tired face and work-reddened hands, but she held herself straight and did her best to dress neatly.

"Hi," he replied. "Don't I get a present?"

"It's there by your plate. I'm sorry it couldn't be more, but anyhow it's something you need."

He pulled the thin red ribbon off the package on the table. Inside was a white shirt and a cheap necktie. He tried to hide his disappointment. Didn't she know white shirts were only for jerks and that nobody wore neckties any more?

"Thanks," he said. "They're real nice."

She brought him his oatmeal and gave him a hug. "Fourteen!" she murmured. "I declare it's a scandal how boys do grow up!"

Sometimes she talked like that. Southern talk, Rick guessed. She came from a little one-horse Carolina town on what she called the "Outer Banks." That was where she had met the boys' father, when he was stationed on the island with the Coast Guard.

"The shirt an' tie aren't all your presents," Mrs. Landon said. "Here's two dollars. I heard the rodeo was over at Madison Square Garden, an' I guess the two dollars'll get you in, come Saturday."

Rick's face brightened up at that. "Gee, Ma," he answered, "I'd sure like to go. All the top riders'll be there!"

By eight o'clock, he and Joey were on their way to school. It was only four blocks and they had plenty of time, so they dawdled along the way. Soon Rick saw a friend of his, Ziggy Musser, coming along the sidewalk behind them.

14

"Go on," he told Joey peremptorily. "I want to talk to Ziggy."

His younger brother departed, and Rick waited for the approaching boy. They didn't speak, but each gave the other the secret signal of the Prospect Owls, the "club" to which they had recently been admitted. The Owls owned the territory for five blocks around P.S. 68, and trespassers from others gangs could be sure of a fight.

"You got any money?" Rick asked.

"Sure," Ziggy grinned. "A coupla bucks—but for me, not for you."

"I don't want it. Just wondered if you felt like goin' t' school today."

"Not me!" Ziggy snorted. "Not today nor any day."

"Okay, why'n't we go over the bridge an' hang around Madison Square Garden? Then we can take in the night rodeo show. Ma gave me the dough."

"Nah," said Ziggy. "Who wants to see cowboys if they ain't havin' a gunfight? Besides, my ol' man'll skin me if I ain't in by his bedtime, an' that's ten-thoity."

Rick went on to school, waited till most of the others were inside, and then ducked around the corner when he thought nobody was looking. He made his way over to Prospect Park and spent the morning heaving pebbles at the squirrels and keeping out of sight of policemen.

He had no notion of waiting till Saturday to see the rodeo. Around noon he boarded a subway train bound for Manhattan.

When he reached the huge building that housed the nation's most famous sports arena, he was disappointed. From the front it looked blank and empty. Slowly he walked around the structure. Near one of the rear doors a lanky young man sat on the curb, and with a quickened pulse Rick recognized him as a genuine cowhand. His sombrero was tilted back on his head, and he held a high-

15

heeled Texas boot in one hand while he rubbed polish on it with the other.

Rick came to stand near him, drinking in every fascinating detail of his dress, from the embroidered tan shirt and calfskin vest to the faded, tight-fitting Levi's. He even noticed that there was a hole in the toe of the man's sock. Finally he got up nerve enough to speak.

"Hi, mister," he said huskily. "You one o' the rodeo riders?"

The cowboy looked up with a grin. "Howdy, son," he replied. "Yeah—reckon ye might call me that—but I ain't enjoyed much luck at it here so far."

"What do you do?" Rick asked.

"Little of everythin'. Bronc-ridin'—steer-wrestlin'—calf-ropin'. Judges are tough here in New York, though. I had a couple o' real good bareback rides an' got disqualified both times. Claimed my feet wasn't high enough, comin' out o' the chute. Heck—I thought they was clean up above the bronc's withers! Anyhow, I ain't made a cent o' prize money yet."

"Gosh," said Rick sympathetically. "That's too bad. I guess you're from Texas, aren't you?"

"Nope. I work on a spread down in Florida. Born an' raised there."

Rick's face must have shown his disappointment.

"That ain't unusual," the cowboy hastened to explain, as he pulled on his boot. "Lots o' cattle ranches in Florida, an' some mighty good riders, too. They's four or five of us here in the Garden."

"I'm comin' to the show tonight," said Rick. "If you're ridin', I'll sure pull for you."

"Thanks, kid," said the man solemnly. "I'm goin' to be workin' my ropin' horse in a few minutes. Mebbe I kin git ye in, if ye'd like."

16

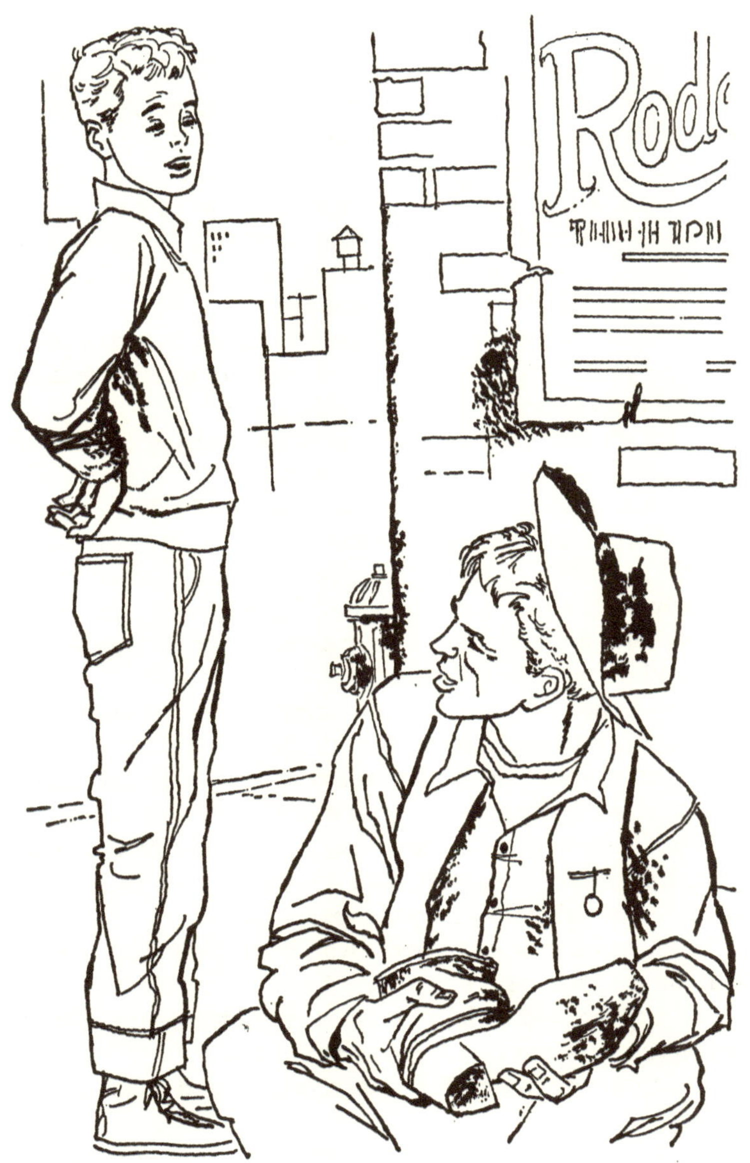
Rode

"Gee! You bet I would. My name's Rick Landon. What's yours?"

"Elmer Jukes is my christened name. What they call me on the circuit is Okeechobee Slim—jus' Slim fer short. Come on—let's talk to the old guy at the door."

The crusty-looking individual guarding the rear entrance gave Rick a cold eye, but Slim marched on in confidently.

"Pete," he said cheerfully, "this here's my nephew. My sister's kid, name o' Rick Landon. I aim to git in some practice, an' he kin help me saddle up."

The doorman stared suspiciously at Rick but finally let them in with a grudging nod. They went up a ramp that led toward the vast interior of the building.

"Stable's over this-a-way," said Slim, steering the boy to the right. At once they were in a different world. Strong, pungent animal smells came to Rick's nostrils. They passed pens of white-face calves, stoutly built box stalls where outlaw horses with wicked, rolling eyes and shaggy coats stood sullenly, and other stalls filled with longhorns and great savage Brahma bulls. Then they came to the section where the saddle stock was quartered.

"Here she is," the cowboy announced. "Sweet Sue. Smartest little ropin' horse east o' the Mississippi."

He rubbed her sleek chestnut coat with a loving hand, then took a Mexican saddle from a long peg on the wall.

"Saddle cloth first," he told Rick. "Smooth it so there's no wrinkles. Then the saddle, like so. An' we'll cinch it up good. 'At a girl, Sue—let yer breath out."

From another peg he took a well-worn lariat and coiled it at the saddle horn. Then he put the mare's bridle on.

"Okay," he said. "Goin' to practice a little ropin'. Think ye kin run as fast as a good frisky range calf?"

"I dunno," answered Rick uncertainly. "I'm game to try, though."

They went out to one end of the tanbark-floored arena

and Slim mounted. "Go ahead," he said. "Run yer darndest, an' duck an' twist all ye want. I promise not to hurt ye, an' I'll give ye a good head start."

Rick darted off at top speed. He had gone twenty yards when he heard the quick pound of hoofs behind him. Then with startling suddenness he felt his arms gripped to his sides, and he was jerked backward, landing with a jarring thump on his back. Seconds later the cowboy was kneeling above him.

"Good enough!" Slim chuckled. "If I'd had my piggin' string, you'd ha' been tied by three legs now, an' I'd ha' set a record."

He loosened the noose that held Rick's arms and helped him to his feet. Ten yards away Sweet Sue stood like a statue, her feet braced to hold the rope taut.

Rick wasn't asked to play calf again. For the next two hours he watched Slim and a few of the other riders work out. Afterward he sat in a corner of the stable on an overturned bucket and listened to their talk. Most of it was about horses, bulls, and steers—the competition stock they would be encountering that evening.

"Hope I draw Ol' Horny in the saddle-bronc ridin'," said a fresh-faced young fellow from Oklahoma. "He sunfishes right purty, an' anybody sticks long enough to make the horn gen'ally gits him a good score."

"You worked that blue roan yet, the one they call Satan's Child?" Slim asked. "Talk about sunfishin'—boy, he'll buck four directions to oncet!"

A little after five, Rick thought he had better be going. He had eaten no lunch, and by now he was hungry.

"Hol' on, now," Slim told him. "You got money fer a ticket tonight?"

"Ma gave me two bucks for my birthday," Rick replied. "But I want somethin' to eat first."

"Shucks," said Slim. "Come an' eat with me. Then I'll

try sneakin' ye in again, an' ye kin save the dough. 'Course, ye won't have a seat, but I reckon ye kin hang 'round the chutes an' act like ye was helpin'. Mebbe ye'll bring me some luck."

They went to a hamburger place around the corner, ate heartily, and returned to Madison Square Garden well before show time. On the way, Slim stopped at his rooming house and dug out a battered old ten-gallon hat, which he put on Rick's head. It came down over his ears, but that made little difference. He looked—or hoped he looked—like a smallish cowhand.

The disguise worked, though there was a different door-keeper on duty this time. Slim nodded familiarly to the man, mumbled something about "my nephew from the ranch," and in they went.

Everything was bustle and confusion now. The riders were edgy as their ordeal drew closer. They adjusted their gear, curried their roping horses, smoked and paced, and had little to say to one another. Out at the side of the arena the bucking horses were being put in the chutes, where most of them stood patiently enough. They knew what was coming and saved their energy till they felt the hated man-legs on their sides.

The thousands of seats, rising tier on tier, began to fill up. Meanwhile, the riders were drawing lots for position and mount. Bareback bronc-riding would be the first event. Slim strolled up to Rick, where he stood near the chutes.

"Wal," he said, with a tight grin, "keep yer fingers crossed. I'm first out, on that mean outlaw Ol' Horny. An' boy, this time they'll see daylight under my boots!"

Chapter Two

The public-address system began to blare overhead. "First event of the evening, ladies and gentlemen—the bareback riding contest. These riders will match their skill against some of the wildest untamed horses of the West. Keep your eyes on Gate Number One. You'll be seeing Okeechobee Slim on Old Horny—ridden only once at this rodeo."

Rick saw Slim let himself down gently onto the shaggy back. He took the single rein from the hackamore in his left hand, pulled his hat down firmly, and raised his right arm. As the gate opened, the big brown horse seemed to explode. He shot out in a long leap, landed stiff-legged, dropped his head, and began to buck, twisting his body to right and left in the air. Rick had been watching Slim's feet as he left the chute. The spurred heels looked high enough at that instant. Now they were raking back and forth across the angry horse's flanks. Once the boy thought his friend's ride was finished as he was tossed a foot above Old Horny's arching spine, but by a miracle he stayed aboard. At eight seconds the horn sounded. Slim had made it!

Another rider sped alongside and dragged him off while the outlaw kept on bucking. There was a brief delay, with the judges adding up their points. Then the announcer's voice boomed out again. "One hundred and seventy-two!"

it said. "A mighty good score for you other riders to shoot at!"

Slim came back and grabbed Rick by the shoulder. "Didn't I say ye'd bring me luck?" He laughed. "Stick around, kid!"

No other rider topped the Florida cowboy's score. The nearest was a one-sixty-nine, compiled by a sawed-off veteran from Montana on Satan's Child. Slim took the five hundred dollars of first-prize money.

Calf-roping was next on the program, and Slim was scheduled to go out twelfth in a field of seventeen. He took Rick over to the pen for a look at his calf. It was a rangy crossbreed, more brindle than red.

"Goin' to need plenty more luck on this one," said Slim dubiously. "Them long-legged critters is fast an' hard to throw."

The event was already in progress, with one rider after another speeding out after a calf. The best time, up to the moment Slim was called, was ten and two-tenths seconds.

"Now," the announcer intoned, "coming out of Gate Twelve—Okeechobee Slim."

The tall cowboy was in the saddle, the pigging string held in his teeth, and Sweet Sue waited, trembling a little. Her eyes were bright and her ears pricked forward. She knew this was her big moment. As the calf dashed out and the barrier dropped, she took off in pursuit like a scared cat. Slim's arm went up, whirling the rope. The calf veered in front of him and he let it fly.

Rick saw the loop settle neatly over the animal's head, but what happened next was so fast he could barely follow it. Slim had landed running. He raced down the rope, caught the floundering calf by a hind leg, tossed it on its back, and whipped the string around three legs in a perfect hog-tie. As he straightened, lifting his hands, the announcer spoke excitedly.

22

"The time," he cried, "was seven and four-tenths seconds —a new record for the event here in the Garden!"

Nobody else came close. Slim placed only sixth in the saddle-bronc riding contest, missed entirely in the steer-wrestling, and was thrown before the horn sounded when he tried to ride a Brahma bull. But his two firsts gave him top money for the night.

"Dunno what I'd ha' done without you, kid," he told Rick when it was over. "Mebbe you oughta stick around an' be my mascot!"

The youngster would have like nothing better, but now it was nearly eleven o'clock and he knew he was in for trouble if he didn't hurry home. He thanked Slim and ran for the subway.

The street door of the old apartment house was unlocked.

When he had climed two flights, Rick took off his shoes and went up on tiptoe, hoping his mother was asleep. A line of light came dimly from under the door. He turned the knob cautiously and crept in.

"Where've you been, Ricky?" asked Mrs. Landon quietly. She sat there in a chair in the narrow hall. Under the bare overhead light her face looked gray and pinched with weariness.

"Mr. Buck was here—the truant officer," she went on before he had time to think up a story. "He says you didn't go to school at all today."

There wasn't much he could do but tell the truth. "I went to the rodeo," he said sullenly. "Heck—who wants to go to school on his birthday? I just couldn't see waitin' till Saturday. It didn't cost me anything, though—only subway fare. A cowpuncher took me in an' I helped him practice ropin'. Here's your two bucks back."

She shook her head sadly. "No, Rick, it's yours. I thought, big as you are, an' fourteen years old, I could begin to depend on you. But you seem to get wilder an' more disobedient every day. Go to bed now, an' don't wake Joey if you can help it."

He crawled miserably into bed. All the magical thrill of that afternoon and evening seemed to have gone sour. He knew he had done wrong, and it made him angry at himself, at his mother, and at the world in general.

*   *   *

The crowd at school took little interest in his account of his adventure. They guffawed loudly when he told about doubling for a calf and refused to believe he had had any part in helping a rider win top money in the night's performance. When Ziggy Musser called him a liar, he punched him in the nose, and as a consequence he was hauled up before the principal. All in all, it was a bad day.

24

Rick was on his way home when he saw several of the bigger boys lounging in front of the ice-cream parlor. Rocky Grattan, leader of the Prospect Owls, was among them. He had hardly deigned to notice Rick before, but now, as he started past, Rocky crooked a finger at him.

"Come here, kid," he said. "You got any dough? Let's see it."

He glanced at the two dollars and nodded. " 'Nough fer a round of shakes. Come on, guys. Young Ricky's treatin'."

There was nothing Rick could do about it, and he felt secretly flattered. It was something to be spoken to by the great Grattan. Big Jake Suchek laid a hand on his shoulder and grinned. "Good kid!" he said hoarsely.

When half a dozen of them had squeezed in around a sticky-topped table and the shakes were set in front of them, Mike Selensky leaned close to Rick and spoke in a low voice.

"Looks like you're really one of the Owls now," he murmured. "Hear you ain't afraid of a fight. We got word how some of the Bridge boys are headin' up this way tonight. You'll want to be in on the rumble, of course."

Rick had a sinking feeling at the pit of his stomach. He knew what a gang rumble was like. Switchblades and zip-guns, brass knuckles and baseball bats. He must have turned pale, for he found the others staring at him coldly.

"Ain't chicken, are you?" Tough Tony Lambretta asked in a hard, quiet voice.

He shook his head and took a pull at the straw in his drink. "Naw," he gulped. "I'll be around."

"Okay," said Tony. "Ten o'clock, over by Louie's pool hall."

Rick's feet dragged as he climbed the steep stairs to the flat. He had so little appetite for supper that his mother worried about him.

"Don't tell me you're coming down sick," she said.

"Maybe what you need is a good dose of castor oil or something."

He pretended to do some homework, his eye straying furtively to the clock every few minutes. At last Mrs. Landon went to bed. It was getting close to ten. He got up, pale and shaky, his mouth dry with fear, stole into the back bedroom, and got an old sock out of the drawer. Then he let himself out as quietly as possible, went down to the back yard, and filled the toe of the sock with gravel. It was the only weapon he could find.

Most people were in bed and it was quiet on the back streets. Light came dimly from the door of the pool parlor. He could see shadows lurking on either side, and as he came closer, they materialized into the dark figures of various Owls. All of them were dressed alike, in jeans and black leather jackets.

"Okay," said Rocky. "Everybody here? We'll move in twos, so's the cops won't get wise. Anybody spots a Bridge Bearcat, give a whistle. Tony, you an' me'll lead off."

Rick found himself paired with Mike Selensky, who carried a tire chain and had a switchblade knife in his pocket. He was somewhat scornful of Rick's homemade blackjack, but it was too late to do anything about it. They had sauntered some two blocks toward Flatbush Avenue when a shrill, peculiar whistle sounded, somewhere ahead.

"That's it!" cried Mike. "Come on, kid!"

A single street light shone down on a dozen youths at the next corner. They were pacing slowly back and forth, hands in pockets. Most of the group were strangers, Rick saw, but Rocky and Tony were there, and other Owls were coming up on the run. Just as they reached the corner, a big fellow with a ducktail haircut gave Tony a sudden shove with his shoulder. Then, with hardly a sound, the fight began.

Things happened too quickly for Rick to follow the tide of battle. He was in the thick of it before he knew just how

26

he got there. He swung his weighted sock at a Bearcat, but the much-darned fabric gave way and the gravel spilled out. He began striking out blindly with his fists. Then he was knocked down himself. Pinned under a sprawling mass of legs and arms, he felt a sudden sharp pain in his left shoulder.

At that moment there was a furious shrilling of police whistles and a scamper of fleeing feet. Before the dazed youngster could scramble up, he was seized by a blue-coated officer.

"Come along wid me, now, an' come quiet," said an ominous Irish voice. "Looks like ye got a bit of a cut, from the bleedin'. Soives ye right, fightin' wid knives an' such. When I was a bye, we managed wid our two hands."

A few minutes later Rick was shoved into a patrol truck along with two other youngsters. One was a stranger, probably a Bridge Bearcat. The other was Mike Selensky. At the nearest precinct they were booked for street-fighting. Then the officer who had arrested him took another and more careful look at Rick's shoulder.

"This bye's got a deep knife cut," he told the sergeant. "He's lost some blood an' we'd better get him to a hospital. It'll do the others good to spend the night in jail."

*   *   *

Rick woke up next morning in a big, white, funny-smelling room, full of beds. His head felt dizzy and there was a tight bandage around his upper arm and shoulder. An overworked nurse took his pulse and temperature. Later she brought him a tray of breakfast and raised the bed so that he was sitting up. Surprisingly, the food tasted good.

At nine o'clock his mother came into the ward, her face sad and strained. She leaned over the cot and kissed him.

"Oh, Ricky, how'd you get mixed up in this nasty business?" she asked with a break in her voice. "Don't try to talk. I know you're hurt, and it's probably my fault. I haven't made a very good home for you, son."

He tried to answer—to tell her he loved her and felt ashamed of himself. But before he could find the words, a big, blue-uniformed young man came to stand beside the cot.

"Officer McClure, mum," said the patrolman, in some embarrassment. "How's the young spalpeen doin' this mornin'?"

"I'm okay," Rick replied. He recognized the officer as the one who had caught him last night, but somehow he felt no resentment. The man had just been doing his job, and he had been pretty decent about it.

"I talked to the floor nurse," said McClure. "Ye'll be discharged before night, she tells me. But I'm sorry to say ye're still under technical arrest. There's the matter of a hearin' in Juvenile Court tomorrer, Saturday, at ten. I'll see ye there, Mrs. Landon—an' yer son."

Rick was allowed to get up and dress after the doctor changed his bandage that afternoon. He walked the twelve blocks home and stopped to see his mother at the little store where she clerked. Somehow, in his misery, he felt closer to her than he had in years. It made him squirm to think that she was blaming herself for the trouble he was in.

Mrs. Landon managed a smile when he walked in. "You're looking more like yourself," she told him. "Joey'll be coming home from school soon, an' you'd better be there to look after him. You might start some potatoes boiling. I'll be home in an hour or so."

There were customers in the store, so he couldn't speak what was in his heart. But that night before bedtime he put his arms around his mother's thin shoulders. "You're okay, Ma," he told her gruffly. "If the judge gives me a chance, I'll try an' act different from now on."

Sessions of the Juvenile Court were held in a modern

building, downtown. Ricky looked around him in some surprise when he and his mother were ushered in. There was no lofty judge's bench—just a big desk in a sunny, pleasant room, with chairs placed comfortably around it. And behind the desk, in judicial robes, sat a quiet gray-haired woman. She looked up, nodded to them, and continued studying the papers in front of her.

After a moment two other people came in. One was Officer McClure. The other, to Rick's amazement, was Miss Vronsky. The judge sat back and took off her glasses.

"This isn't a trial," she said in a gentle voice. "We're here to find out about the trouble in which Richard Landon is involved—what caused it and what can be done about it. I've read your report, officer. Have you anything to add to that?"

The patrolman stood up, twisted his cap in his hands, and cleared his throat. "It was just another gang fight, yer Honor," he said. "Twenty or so young lads, half of 'em from another precinct. This bye here was a new member o' the Prospect Owls. To the best o' my belief this was the first rumble he'd took any part in. One reason he got caught was that some young hood had stuck a knife in him. That's the feller I'd ha' liked to get me hands on."

The black-robed lady nodded and made a note or two. "Now," she said, "what about Richard's school record? I see here that he's been reported often for truancy."

Miss Vronsky sat forward. "Your Honor," she said, "may I put in a word on that? I'm one of Rick's teachers, at P.S. 68. This boy has a good mind. If he doesn't care for school particularly, the school itself may be partly at fault. I think you know what it's like in those old buildings, over-crowded and dark and—well—dismal. Nearly all the boys and girls live in tenements, and the kind of home discipline most of them get doesn't tend to make them very good citizens. I'm sure that doesn't apply in Rick's case, but they're the sort of youngsters he has to associate with. In a different environment I'd expect him to do a great deal better."

"You mean," said the judge with a smile, "you don't have *any* students who enjoy learning?"

"A few," Miss Vronsky replied. "But they're never popular with the other pupils. Children who study are considered 'squares.' "

There was a thoughtful pause. Then the judge turned to Rick. "Well, Richard," she said, "we haven't heard from you. After all, you're fourteen and must have some ideas of your own. What would you like to be when you grow up? Surely not a gangster."

His face felt hot and he squirmed under her calm scrutiny. "No, ma'am," he blurted out at last. "A cowpuncher. Or else a Coast Guardsman like my dad was. Look—I didn't want to get mixed up in that fight the other night. But the Owls is the only outfit I could belong to. If I hadn't gone with 'em, they'd have called me 'chicken.' "

His mother reached over and took his hand. "Your Honor," she said, "I've been thinking hard these last two days. Everything that's been said here this morning makes me surer what I want to do. I was raised on a little island down on the North Carolina coast. It's called Ocracoke. Probably you never heard of the place. Living's cheap there, an' folks are independent. There aren't any gangs, or truant officers, or even policemen. But they've got churches, an' a good school where the youngsters are proud to learn. What I'd like to do is take my two boys an' move down there."

Mrs. Landon bowed her head and waited while the judge sat silent, her eyes on the reports before her.

"In the opinion of this court," she said at length, "you've proposed an interesting solution. I was expecting to put Richard on probation. Frankly, I doubt if it would effect any real cure. If you are prepared to make this move in the next thirty days, I'll suspend sentence and wish you all success."

The lady in the black robes smiled and looked inquiringly at Miss Vronsky and the patrolman.

"I think it's a wonderful idea," said the teacher. "How I'd love to work in a school like that!"

"Yes, yer Honor," McClure chimed in. "It sounds good to me. How they iver get along wid no police is a mystery, but maybe the kids are busy enough other ways to keep 'em out o' mischief."

"Very well," said the judge. "Court dismissed."

Chapter Three

Rick was disturbed at the idea of moving. True, he had never been very happy in Brooklyn, but it was the only home he knew. And Joey, who had spent nearly all his nine years in the walk-up flat, was openly rebellious.

Mrs. Landon, frantically busy trying to tie up the many loose ends and arrange for sending their few household goods to Ocracoke, had little time to reassure the boys. But one night she mentioned something about the island that made a difference in their outlook.

"Heck," Rick had remarked at supper, "what'll there be to do down there? I bet the guys are all too countrified to play stickball or hang around the park or have any kind o' fun."

"Well," said his mother wearily, "they ride, for one thing. When I was a girl, there were a heap o' wild ponies, an' all the boys rode 'em bareback."

Rick's eyes fairly popped. "Honest?" he asked. "Gee, wouldn't that be somethin'! Only that was way back in the olden days, an' they're prob'ly all gone by now."

Mrs. Landon laughed. "I'm not *that* old," she answered. "An' things don't change a whole lot, down there on the Outer Banks. I guess there's still enough ponies to go 'round."

That was the last of May. School wouldn't be out for another two weeks, and Rick was going to school every day now. He didn't like it any better, but he felt he owed that much to Miss Vronsky after the way she had stood by him at the Juvenile Court. Once, when he got to her room early, she opened an atlas and showed him where Ocracoke was. It certainly looked like the tail end of nowhere when you found it on the map.

Over the years Mrs. Landon had managed to put a little more than three hundred dollars in the savings bank. It had been intended for a "rainy day"—hospital expenses if she should get sick, or some other emergency. Now she drew the money out, paid a final month's rent, and gave the landlord notice. She knew she was burning her bridges, but she was determined to see her plan through.

A letter came from her uncle, in Ocracoke, saying there was a small house vacant in the village. It wasn't in very good condition, but some of the neighbors would try to put it in shape before she arrived. Everybody, he wrote, was pleased to hear she was going to bring her boys home.

On the day after school closed, Miss Vronsky came to the flat. She found Rick and his mother deep in paper and string and empty cartons, trying to pack up their belongings, and at once she pitched in to help. The things they had were pitifully few and old. There were two beds, a table and a dresser, three or four chairs, and the set of china Mrs. Landon had received as a wedding present. Those and the bedding and kitchen utensils would have to go by freight. The family's clothes were packed in two battered old suitcases.

At noon everything was out and the flat neatly swept. They went to the bus terminal, Miss Vronsky and Mrs. Landon lugging one suitcase between them, Rick carrying the other, and Joey bringing up the rear with two shoe boxes full of sandwiches to be eaten on the way.

The long silvery bus to Washington, Richmond, and the South was ready to take on passengers. They said good-by to Miss Vronsky, and as Rick started to climb aboard, he was embarrassed at having the teacher plant a kiss on his cheek.

"Write to me," she called after him, "and tell me all about your wonderful island!"

Mrs. Landon and the boys got seats together near the rear of the bus. It rolled smoothly out of the terminal, silent except for an occasional hiss of air brakes. There was a long trip through a tunnel under the Hudson, and soon they were out in the open air again, moving with the traffic along the New Jersey Turnpike. Once they pulled clear of the refineries and factories Rick sat fascinated, staring at the green countryside. He had never been out of the city before.

"Hey—look, Ma!" cried Joey. "Those big animals in the park there—what are they?"

"They're just cows, Joey. And it isn't a park. It's a farm. You'll see lots of farms an' plenty of cows before we get where we're going."

It was five o'clock when they reached Baltimore, and nearly dark before they pulled out of Washington, after an hour's stop. The family sat on a bench in the terminal and ate their supper out of one of the shoe boxes.

Through the night they rolled on southward. The bus was air-conditioned and cool. The seats tilted back, and the boys slept while their mother sat quiet, trying not to worry too much about the change she was making in their lives. She had a hundred and thirty dollars left in her worn old pocketbook—a frighteningly small sum on which to make a new start. But her faith that she was right was still strong. Somehow, she felt, they would come through.

Late that night, when the bus made another long stop in Richmond, Rick woke up. He leaned over toward his mother sleepily.

"Aren't we there yet?" he asked. "Seems like we've been goin' a heck of a long while."

34

"No, Ricky," she told him. "I guess we're close to half-way, but we have to change buses when we get to Raleigh, come morning. An' it's still a long trip from there. Go back to sleep now."

Just as day was breaking, they reached Raleigh. There was an hour to wait before they could get another bus going down Route 70 toward the coast. Mrs. Landon improved the time by sending the boys to wash themselves and brush their teeth in the men's room. Then they got some orange juice at the lunch counter and ate more of their sandwiches.

The second bus wasn't as big or luxurious as the one they had been on. The seats didn't tilt and there was no air conditioning. As the June morning wore on, it got pretty hot. They kept the windows open and watched the pine woods and the little farms slide by. At New Bern they saw salt water—a broad arm of the sea with boats riding at their moorings.

"Gee," said Joey, "I'd sure like to ride on one o' them."

"You will," his mother replied. "We've got to take a long boat trip after we get off the bus."

They went on through Newport and Beaufort, then swung northeastward till they reached the town of Atlantic, just before noon. There was no time for lunch then. The mailboat *Marlin* would be leaving for the Outer Banks at twelve-thirty. Sweating under the weight of the suitcases, they made their way down the street toward the dock. A rich, ripe smell of fish and shrimp and oysters assailed their nostrils as they passed the packing houses and piers. And the talk that came to Rick's ears was like nothing he had ever heard—the soft, slurring accents of the South, overlaid with a special manner of speaking that belonged only to natives of the coast.

Captain Burnham was waiting at the gangplank, watch in hand. " 'Bout ready to cast off," he told Mrs. Landon.

"This all o' yer luggage? Moight's well go roight on aboard. Say—ain't you Annie Howard, from Ocracoke?"

Her face brightened and she laughed. "Used to be," she answered. "First time I've been home for fifteen years, an' it's good to hear folks talk like you. These are my two boys, Cap'n. Our name's Landon now."

"Sho' 'nough," he nodded. "I mind me now. You married young Dick Landon. Heard he got killed a while back. Too bad."

He gave them a hand with the bags, and they took their seats on benches under an awning toward the stern, where four or five other passengers were gathered. Promptly at twelve-thirty a bell jangled, the engine began to chug more loudly, and the *Marlin* backed away from the dock.

For about five minutes the boys were content to sit and look out at the harbor shoreline. Then, in spite of their mother's warnings, they were scampering all over the boat. The *Marlin* was a forty-five footer, broad in the beam and seaworthy. At the moment the water was calm enough, but Pamlico Sound can kick up some big waves in a storm, and the boat was built to take them.

Rick soon made friends with the deck hand. "What is this we're on, a river?" he asked.

"Nope," the man replied, spitting over the rail. "This yer's the mouth o' Core Sound. Atlantic's in Carteret County—more or less part o' the mainland. Over yon to the east'ard is Portsmouth Island. 'Fore long we'll be out in the Big Sound—Pamlico, that is. You ever been on a boat before?"

"Well," said Rick, "I rode the ferry to Staten Island once. It only took about twenty minutes, though. How long's it take you to get to Ocracoke?"

"Round about four hours. 'Tain't but thirty-foive or forty mile, but we make a stop to put mail off at Portsmouth."

36

Up in the pilothouse the captain was steering his craft carefully, skirting the buoys that marked the windings of the channel. He seemed unconcerned when Rick climbed up beside him.

"How do they call you, son?" he asked.

"Richard Landon, Junior," said Rick. "Did you know my dad?"

"Sho' did. A foine young man, yer dad. He was with the Coast Guard at Ocracoke. Reckon he met yer ma there."

"I don't think I'm goin' to like it much," Rick volunteered. "We're city people. I guess Ocracoke must be a pretty hick kind of a place."

Captain Burnham nodded. "She ain't a metropolis; that's a fact," he said mildly. "The boys there seem to do pretty good, though. Don't ever hear 'em complainin' much. Mebbe you better go below an' set down, son. We're gittin' out in the Sound an' the sea's pickin' up."

Rick didn't like taking orders, but he had noticed that the deck was heaving up and down under him and his stomach was a little uneasy. He staggered aft to his mother and sat down beside her on the bench, feeling as if he might be sick any moment. Joey's face, too, was pale and miserable. Mrs. Landon looked at the pair of them and smiled.

"If you're going to live on an island," she said, "you'll have to get used to a little rough water. I know how it hits you the first time, though."

After a while Rick stumbled to the rail and got rid of it. He began to feel better. Perhaps he wasn't going to die after all. They had been cruising northward for close to three hours when the *Marlin* turned her nose toward the distant shore of Portsmouth Island. On the other side, to port, there was nothing in sight but water, stretching away to the horizon.

Half a mile from shore the engine slowed down and the

mailboat came nearly to a stop. Looking ahead, Rick saw a small rowboat bobbing on the waves. In it was a colored man who stood up amidships as they drifted close.

"Hi, Henry," called the captain. "Ain't got much mail for you today. Folks all well, ashore?"

"Fair, Cap'n, fair to middlin'," the Negro replied with a grin. He poled the skiff alongside and took the small sack of mail passed to him by the deck hand. Then he waved good-by and started back to the island.

"Henry comes out for the mail and supplies every day," Rick's mother explained. "He's been doing it ever since I was a girl. The water's too shallow for a big boat to get in, an' there's only a few folks live there nowadays, anyhow. Whatever they need from the mainland, he takes ashore for 'em."

The *Marlin* got under way again, and soon the water grew rougher as they crossed the wide opening of Ocracoke Inlet.

"That's the Atlantic Ocean," said Mrs. Landon. "Nothing out there but salt water for three thousand miles—all the way to Spain."

At the moment the boys were much too preoccupied with their queasy stomachs to pay attention to her remarks. Once they were past the inlet, however, the boat steadied again. Rick had recovered enough to stare at the southern tip of the island that was to be his home. It didn't look like much —just some bare sand dunes with gulls flying over them. Then, after a few miles, trees appeared, and the roofs of houses nestling among them. He saw the tall white shaft of a lighthouse.

It was after four o'clock when the mailboat swung in past the Coast Guard station and chugged across the little horseshoe-shaped harbor, known as Silver Lake.

"Well, folks," called Captain Burnham cheerily, "here we are in Ocracoke!"

38

Chapter Four

The boat pulled in alongside a rickety-looking little dock and was made fast. At once the other passengers crowded to the side and stepped ashore from the rocking craft. The Landons followed, weighed down by their suitcases.

Rick's first look at the place was hardly reassuring. They sure had a nerve, he thought, to call this dump a town. There was a road of sorts, running around the little harbor, where, at other piers, small, dirty-looking fishing boats were tied up. Most of the houses were small, too, and all built of wood. Some were weather-beaten, in need of paint. Standing in the road near the tiny post office were a few cars and jeeps, nearly all of them old and rusty.

The one thing there seemed to be plenty of was people. There must have been fifty of them gathered there to see the boat come in and pick up the mail. All of them—men and women, boys and girls—had a sunburned, healthy look. Most of the men were roughly clad in khaki pants and T-shirts, but he did see several girls in pretty cotton dresses. The boys looked like boys anywhere.

Suddenly, before they reached the shoreward end of the dock, a big, tanned, gray-haired man in a fisherman's jersey came hurrying to meet them.

"That you, Annie?" he asked with a grin. "Sho' has been a long toime, but Oi'd know you anywheres. These the boys?"

He gave Mrs. Landon a hearty kiss and stuck out a brawny hand to shake Rick's.

"This is my Uncle Dan Howard," their mother told the boys. "I guess he's about the nearest kinfolks you've got in the world."

"The house you're goin' to live in," Uncle Dan explained, "is back over to the east'ard. 'Tain't very fur from the school an' the church. Neighbors have been fixin' it up a little. Oi got the car here, so we kin roide over."

On the way to the automobile half a dozen other people greeted Mrs. Landon, and she stopped to talk to them. As a consequence, it was a good half hour later when they rattled up a narrow dirt road, overhung by trees, and stopped in front of a dilapidated picket fence. Behind it stood a little two-story frame house.

"Yoohoo, Annie!" a voice sang out, and on the wooden steps they saw a plump woman in an apron waving a welcome. Behind her the doorway was crowded with other women, all laughing and calling greetings. Rick would have been more impressed by this neighborly display if his eyes hadn't chanced to stray down the lane. There, cropping grass beside the fence, was a horse!

It was a smallish horse, rough-coated but well built. Its long foretop hung down over its eyes, and there were cockleburrs in its matted mane and tail. Rick stood there staring, his mouth agape.

"Look, Ma!" he half whispered. "Is that one o' the wild ponies?"

She didn't hear him, for she was already the center of a chattering group. Uncle Dan was carrying the suitcases to the door and Joey was with him. Rick went a few steps nearer the little horse. It looked up, tossed its head, snorted once, and trotted off down the lane till it disappeared around a bend.

By that time Rick had been missed. He heard a big, hearty voice calling him. "Come here, boy, an' say howdy to these good folks."

There were more Howards among the welcomers, also a number of Styrons and O'Neals. These seemed to be common names on the island, and many were related to each other. Rick was so busy meeting them and being shown over the house that he forgot about the pony for the moment.

Their new home had been scrubbed from top to bottom, and there were neatly ironed curtains at the front windows. On the first floor there was a fair-sized living room with a large kitchen behind it. Up the steep, narrow stairway there were two bedrooms. Somewhat to Rick's puzzlement there was no bathroom, but he soon found out the purpose of the little wooden structure half hidden behind a yaupon bush at the back of the yard.

Since the Landons' furniture would be at least another week in arriving, the neighbors had installed two old beds, a table, and three chairs. There were enough pots and pans to take care of simple cooking, and eggs, flour, sugar, and other staples had been put on the kitchen shelves. Besides that, the good ladies of the village had brought two loaves of bread, some homemade jam, and half a ham. An iron pump at one end of the sink supplied the house with water.

Uncle Dan beckoned to the boys. "I reckon the firewood'll be one o' your jobs," he said. "That's a good cookstove, an' she'll work foine, long's you keep the wood box full. Ever learn to use an ax or a bucksaw?"

Rick shook his head. As far as he knew, he had never even seen such tools.

"Come out here an' watch me," said the older man. He took a four-foot log from the woodpile, laid it across a

rickety sawhorse, and sawed it into three even lengths. Then
he set one chunk on end, lifted the ax, and split it cleanly
down the middle.

"Them two halves," he said, "would be all roight fer
keepin' a foire overnight. Fer a quick foire, or fer kindlin',
ye'd jest split it foiner—loike this."

With three or four quick strokes he reduced the half
log to smaller sticks, then stood by while Rick had a try at
it. He was pretty clumsy at first. Then, with Uncle Dan's
encouragement, he began to do better. Joey meanwhile,
was carrying the split sticks inside and filling the wood
box in the kitchen.

All the neighbors had departed when Rick came in,
mopping the sweat from his face. His mother was getting
supper.

"Gosh," the boy growled, "what a jerk joint! No gas an'
no 'lectric light! Nothin' but wood to burn. I bet I'm goin'
to have to work all the time!"

Mrs. Landon laughed. "Oh, I don't know as it'll hurt
you," she said. "We'll get some coal, soon as we can
afford it, an' maybe we can have electricity put in some
day. Meantime, I reckon we can get along the way I did as
a girl. Here's the washbasin. Clean yourself up for supper
now. An' you'd better watch how you speak, or the folks
here'll think you talk mighty funny."

"Me?" He was shocked at the idea. "It's these Ocracokers that talk funny. They say 'Oi loike it all roight.'
What kind o' hick lingo is that?"

His mother turned and gave him a look that silenced him.
"It isn't how people talk that counts," she said. "It's what's
in their hearts. These folks are kind an' friendly. Look
what they've done for us."

Joey came in by the time supper was ready. His eyes
were shining with new discoveries. "I like this place, Ma,"
he chirped. "I saw a cow an' some hens—right here on this

street! An' there was a horse, too, but he ran off. There's a boy named Abel in the next house. He promised to take me fishin' with him."

Rick made no comment, but he resolved to do some exploring for himself before dark. Meanwhile, he had really enjoyed his meal. It was the first home-baked bread he had ever tasted, and he ate four slices, spread with fig preserve.

When he went out again, the sun was still bright in the west. Once more he looked at the house, this time with a less critical eye. Like many other buildings in Ocracoke, it had no basement but rested on short, solid cement piles. As he found out later, this was to prevent damage when a high storm tide washed over the island. There were newly made screens at the doors and windows, and the roof was speckled in spots where it had been patched with fresh shingles. To Rick, a roof should be a flat area of tin and tar. This one, with its evidence of helpful activity by the neighbors, failed to impress him.

He wandered on down the lane, passed two or three other houses, and came to a path that forked off to the right into a thicket of cedar and wax myrtle. Rick hesitated a moment, for woods were something he knew very little about. But when he heard a faint snort and a thud of hoofs, he hurried forward along the path.

The sounds came nearer, and Rick looked eagerly toward the bend, a few yards ahead. Suddenly a galloping horse appeared. It wasn't the one he had seen earlier. This pony was lighter-colored—a chestnut with a blond mane and tail—and on its back rode a boy about Rick's own age.

As he drew abreast, the young rider gave a tug on his mount's mane and brought it to a stop.

"Hoi," he said. "Reckon you're the new feller from the city. Moy name's Jed Rowan. What's yours?"

"Rick Landon. Yeah, we just got here today. Is that one o' the wild ponies I've heard about?"

"Well, they're not exactly woild," Jed replied with a grin. "We jes' call 'em Banker ponies. They run loose, but most all of 'em are branded an' belong to somebody. We got a mounted Boy Scout troop—only one in the East, so folks say. This is one o' the troop ponies. You aim to live here an' go to school an' all?"

At the word "school" Rick stopped smiling. "Yeah," he grumbled. "I guess so."

"Bet you loike it in our school," Jed told him. "We do, anyhow. Well, so long now."

He kicked his bare heels into the pony's ribs and dashed off down the woods road. Rick looked after him, full of envy, then turned and went farther along the trail. Big, gnarled live oaks overhung the narrow path. In the loose sand were tracks—the dainty oval prints of pony hoofs. Overhead, somewhere in a tree, a mockingbird sang lustily. And something of these new sights and sounds crept into the city boy's heart. He felt a kind of pleasure he had never known before.

Rick had gone about a quarter of a mile when he came to a little cemetery on a rise of ground among the trees. Like the dooryards it was surrounded by a fence, and in it were perhaps a dozen stones, stained with age and lichen-covered. These were the graves of long-dead Howards. Stealing inside, he peered at some of the names, and on one stone he could make out the inscription:

In Memory of
ANN HOWARD
Wife of George Howard
Born—1724
Died November 24, 1841
Aged 117 Years

Ann Howard! That was his own mother's maiden name. And this woman, undoubtedly an ancestor of theirs, had lived her long life here more than a century ago.

Not far away was another small enclosure containing only four graves. These were more recent. From the bronze marker he found that the men buried there were British sailors from a ship of war torpedoed off Ocracoke by a German submarine in World War II. Tattered, faded little British flags stood at the graves' heads, and one had fallen over. Rick picked it up and replanted it where it belonged.

On the way home in the gathering dusk he met two more of the ponies. One was a half-grown colt with a short, fuzzy tail. It shied away from him and nuzzled against its mother, who passed so close to Rick that he could touch her brown side. Somewhere off in the darkness a whip-poorwill called. The eerie, throaty whistle sent a tingle down the boy's back. He hurried homeward, listening with a mixture of pleasure and fear to the noises of unknown wild things in the woods.

Before bedtime Mrs. Landon insisted that both her sons take a bath in the washtub near the stove. Then they crawled into the bed they were to share. It had been a long, exciting day. Joey dropped off, and within five minutes Rick, too, was fast asleep.

Chapter Five

"Get in a good big armful o' wood, Rick," said his mother at breakfast. "I've got a lot o' washing to do, an' I'll need to heat water. When that's done, you can run an errand for me, down to the Community Store. It's right close to the post office an' the mailboat dock, where we landed yesterday. Here's some money an' a list o' the things I need. Don't dawdle on the way. Joey, you stay an' help me."

Rick was beginning to get the hang of the village's geography, and he had no trouble finding the road that skirted Silver Lake. There were half a dozen customers in the store when he got there. Four were Ocracoke housewives, doing their marketing. The other two were a man and woman in expensive-looking sports clothes. They oh'd and ah'd over some of the assorted merchandise, picked out things to take home as souvenirs, and exclaimed, "How quaint!" when they found something they liked. Evidently they were tourists from the North. Rick was sure of it when he saw them drive off in a shiny new convertible.

The Ocracokers smiled among themselves. "Them off-oislanders sho' got queer notions," said one of them. She turned and noticed Rick.

"You mus' be Ann Howard's boy," she said. "How you loike it here, so fur?"

"It's okay, I guess," he replied. "Maybe I'll get used to it after a while."

The woman nodded understandingly. "Mus' be a moighty big change fer you," she said and went back to her shopping.

When he had been waited on, Rick picked up the big bag of groceries and started out. There had been candy and bottles of pop that tempted him, but he knew the family hadn't much money. As he went down the steps, a pony trotted up and Jed Rowan swung down from its back.

"Hoi, Rick," came his greeting. "Looks heavy. Want a roide home?"

"Gee!" said Rick, pleased at the idea. "Can he carry the two of us?"

"Naw—but you git on an' hold the sack. Oi'll lead him."

At least Rick knew which side to mount. He scrambled awkwardly to the pony's back, gripping the narrow body with his legs. The pony snorted and tossed its head.

"Ain't used to bein' rid by anybody with shoes on." Jed laughed. "Here's yer groceries. Jest hang on now. I won't let him run."

He took a fistful of the little horse's mane, just behind the ears, and set off at a walk, the pony following obediently. By the time they reached the Landon house, Rick thought that riding horseback was easy.

"Got chores to do or somethin'?" Jed asked. "If you ain't, Oi could show you the place."

Rick took the bag inside, where his mother was busy over the washboard. She told him he might go with the Rowan boy if he would put up the clothesline in the back yard first. With Jed's help he quickly strung it between a post at the rear and an old live oak tree beside the house.

"We'll go afoot," said Jed. He gave the pony a slap on the rump and it ambled off down the lane. The boys set off in the other direction.

"Yon's the school," said Jed. "Back this side is where we

48

play ball, recess-toime. 'Tain't much of a ball field—jest
sand—but we git a lot o' fun out of it. This buildin's our
recreation hall. They have square dances here, 'bout oncet
a week. An' over there's the Meth'dist Church. You a
Meth'dist?"

"Search me," Rick answered. "I never went to church
much, but I guess Ma used to be one when she lived down
here. Say, tell me—why do all the houses have a fence
around 'em?"

"They're to keep ponies out o' the flower beds an' veg'-
table gardens," Jed explained. "Used to be hogs an' cattle
runnin' loose, too, but since there's been cars on the oiland,
that ain't allowed."

They made a circuit around the front of a big frame
building that Jed said was the Wahab Village Hotel.
"That's where some o' the tourists stay. A lot of 'em come
here to fish or hunt or jes' plain loaf. This part o' the hotel's
where we have movie shows every Sat'day noight."

They swung westward toward the harbor. "You've seen
the north side," said Jed. "Let's go down southerly, past
the loighthouse." He pointed out the Coast Guard station,
across the water, and the long, many-colored building that
housed the garage and marine engine repair shop, and the
headquarters of the National Park Service.

"Most o' the oiland's gov'ment land now," he said. "All
but the village is part o' Cape Hatt'ras National Seashore
Park. Our ranger's a good feller, though. Gits along real
foine with the folks here."

Now they bore to the left, with the tall shaft of the
lighthouse straight ahead. On their right were several docks,
and a boat was tied to one of them. Its engine began chugging as they passed.

"That's Hank Styron's boat," said Jed. "He's gittin' ready
to take some tourists out fishin'."

They turned left again to the east of the lighthouse. Rick

stopped and stared at a thick, strangely patterned tree trunk, topped by a ragged fringe of fronds. "Gee," he said, "that looks sort o' like pictures I've seen. What is it?"

"It's a palm tree," Jed told him proudly. "She's pretty old an' moth-et now, but there ain't another one growin' this fur north, so they say. We got plenty o' Spanish bayonet around, too, an' fig trees. Oi seen one in your yard. Figs ought to be ripe fer pickin' a couple o' weeks from now."

The lighthouse, in its neat, white-fenced plot, had a look of age, despite its fresh coat of paint. Rick asked how old it was and was surprised to hear it had stood there since 1823.

"If it wa'n't there," Jed said, "Oi reckon we'd have even more shipwrecks'n we do. 'Most every big storm, there'll be a vessel poile up on the shoals along Ocracoke an' Hatt'ras. Gives the Coast Guard aplenty to do."

He led Rick along a little sand road that soon turned southwestward. "You ever heered o' Blackbeard, the poirate?" he asked.

"Sure, I read about him in a book once."

"Well," said Jed impressively, "he's prob'ly stood roight here. Springer's Point, where we're goin', is the place ol' Teach—that was Blackbeard's real name—used to have his hideout. Folks say he anchored out there offshore, in what they call Teach's Hole. Then him an' his men would row in to the beach. It's pretty much out o' soight o' the village, an' the two or three families that lived on the island never dared to bother him anyhow. Oi don't fault 'em fer that. Him an' his crew was pretty rough."

"Hey!" Rick exclaimed. "I bet there's treasure buried 'round here! Me—I'm goin' to dig some of it up!"

Jed laughed. "Wisht Oi had a nickel fer every shovelful o' sand that's been dug lookin' fer it," he said. "Not a moite of it's ever been found, or prob'ly ever will be."

50

Rick was unconvinced. He looked around at the sand and brush and yuccas with a greedy eye. Where pirates had been, there must be gold. That was something about Ocracoke his mother hadn't told him. Before too long he meant to bring a shovel down here.

"Look," said Jed as they walked back toward the lighthouse. "It's a whoile yet till noon. Want to go over to the ocean an' see the beach? You better leave them shoes home first, though. All you'll do is git 'em full o' sand."

"Naw," said Rick scornfully. "I've seen beaches before. I bet Coney Island makes this one look sick."

"Coney Oiland?" asked Jed. "Where's that?"

"Right close to Brooklyn at the end o' the el," Rick replied. "Gee, you mean you never heard of it? Saturdays an' Sundays there's a million people on the beach at Coney."

Jed smiled. "Mus' be a little thick fer swimmin'," was all he said.

They parted at a fork in the road near the schoolhouse. Rick didn't feel like going home yet, so he wandered down past the post office and stores. A rumble of big diesels came from the ice and power plant, and he looked through the open door into the dark interior. Farther out on the pier three or four men were packing fish for shipment to the mainland. They grinned at him in friendly fashion, but he went on without talking to them.

Out on the sand flat north of the Coast Guard station, he came to an area where plank tables, benches, and sheet-iron barbecue stoves made it look like a picnic ground. Two or three tents had been set up, and over at the edge of Pamlico Sound he could hear the cheerful voices of swimmers. As he came nearer, he saw a dozen youngsters playing in the sand and thrashing about in the waves. He would like to have joined them, but, he remembered bitterly, he didn't own a pair of bathing trunks. He went off some distance from the others, pulled off his shoes and socks, rolled up his jeans, and waded out into the shallow water.

A huge, awkward-looking white bird was swimming thirty yards away. It looked somewhat like a swan, but uglier. It had a very long bill with a pouch beneath. When it saw him, it took off from the surface of the Sound and flapped away on black-edged wings. The sight of it made him forget to be sorry for himself for a minute. He couldn't be sure, but he thought the bird was a pelican. If he hadn't been afraid of sounding ignorant, he would have asked someone.

When he came out of the water, he didn't bother to put his shoes on. The sand felt surprisingly good to his bare feet as he plodded homeward, and he began to see why the island boys went all summer without shoes.

Hiking along the back road, he saw a jeep pulled up beside the fence in front of his home. Two people were

getting out. One was a wiry gray-haired man with spectacles, a close-cropped mustache, and a boyish grin. The lady with him was shorter and plumper. She too wore glasses, and her face lit up in a smile when she saw Rick.

"Hello," she called. "Are you one of Mrs. Landon's boys?"

"Yes'm," he said. "You looking for my mother?"

"We wanted to meet her, and you, too. We're the Randalls. My husband's principal of the school, and I teach there. Let's go in, if your mother's at home. I brought her some things."

Mrs. Landon had hung out her washing and was in the kitchen when they entered. She dried her reddened hands on her apron and told Rick to pull out chairs for the guests.

"Then go see if you can find Joey," she added.

Rick located his brother in the next yard, playing with Abel Dennis, and dragged the protesting youngster home. In the front room they heard their mother laughing. She sounded happier than she had ever been in Brooklyn, and it gave Rick a pang of envy. This was home to her, in a way he was sure it would never be to him.

"Mr. Randall wanted to know what grades you boys'll be in," she told her sons. "I was saying Joey'd be ready for fourth. An' you finished eighth grade this June, didn't you, Ricky?"

He nodded with little enthusiasm.

"Good!" said the school principal. "We've got some fine boys and girls entering ninth this fall. Jed Rowan, for one. I think I saw you with him this morning, not far from our place—over by the lighthouse. By the way, I brought you a book or two to read. Thought you might like to know more about Ocracoke's history."

"What about the ponies?" Mrs. Randall asked. "Have you ridden one yet?"

"I have!" Joey replied eagerly. "Abel an' I caught one close to his house an' we both rode him."

"I was on Jed Rowan's this morning," Rick put in. "But I guess unless you're a Scout, you don't get much chance to ride."

"Hm," the principal murmured, scratching his chin. "Maybe we could do something about that, eh, Carolyn?"

His wife nodded briskly. "I don't suppose you belonged to a Scout troop where you lived before, did you, Ricky? Most of the boys do, here on Ocracoke. Cap'n Marvin Howard is the man in charge. And Ben O'Neal, of the Coast Guard, runs the Cub Scout program. If you come to our Sunday School, you'll be likely to meet them both."

They said good-by and went rattling off in the sturdy old jeep.

"Mighty nice folks," Mrs. Landon remarked. "They came here after I left the island, but they're good Ocracokers now. Good teachers, too, everybody says."

She showed them the food Mrs. Randall had brought —a home-baked pie and a dozen fat little pan fish known as "spots." She fried some for lunch, and the boys smacked their lips over them.

"You may as well put those shoes away an' save 'em for dress-up times," their mother told them. "Could be you'll pick up a sandspur or two, but it won't be long before your feet are tough."

That afternoon the weather clouded up and it began to rain, with puffs of wind from the southwest. Since it was too wet and raw outdoors to do any more exploring, Rick curled up with one of the books the Randalls had left.

There was a map in one of them showing the whole long chain of the Outer Banks. First, coming down from the north, he found the sixty-five-mile peninsula that began in Virginia and extended all the way down Bodie's Island to Oregon Inlet. On it were such famous places as Kitty

Hawk, the Kill Devil Hills, and Nag's Head. Marked with a star was the monument to the Wright Brothers' historic first flight. And to the westward lay Roanoke Island, where, he read, Sir Walter Raleigh had founded the first English colony in America in 1587. Its settlers disappeared before Raleigh returned, and it became known as the "Lost Colony."

Below Oregon Inlet was the long, narrow strip of Hatteras Island. It was shaped like a backward "L," with Cape Hatteras at the point of the angle. And finally, running southwest from Hatteras Inlet, he located Ocracoke Island.

As he read some of the early history of the area, he began to grow excited. The log of the first Raleigh expedition told how "a fleet of seven vessels, all small however, and capable of entering the inlets of Virginia sounds . . . set sail from Plymouth, England, April 9, 1585. After various adventures that caused delay the fleet passed the Cape Feare on June 23d, and days later came to anchor at Wokokon, southwest of Cape Hatterask."

They had probably landed near the present village of Ocracoke, looking for wood and water. And it was only after leaving "Wokokon" that they went north to explore the places where they meant to settle. Rick had studied enough American history to realize that right here where he now lived, white men had landed nearly twenty-five years before Henry Hudson sailed into New York Bay—thirty-five years before the Pilgrims came ashore at Plymouth Rock!

By 1715 the name of the island had been changed to Occacock, and the colonial government set up a permanent settlement there for the pilots who guided ships through the inlet into Pamlico Sound. Blackbeard and other buccaneers had probably been using the island as a rendezvous even before that date. It was in November,

1718, that Edward Teach—better known as Blackbeard—
came to his bloody end just off the Ocracoke shore. A
Lieutenant Maynard, coming by sea from Virginia, cap-
tured the pirate vessel after a furious battle, and finally
killed the notorious marauder in hand-to-hand combat.

There was a legend on Ocracoke, so the book said, that
when Teach's head had been cut off, his powerful body
had swum seven times around Maynard's ship before it
sank. More likely to be true was the story that the pirate's
head, with pieces of slow match still burning in the thick,
black whiskers, was stuck on the bowsprit of the lieutenant's vessel and carried proudly up to Bath, on the Pamlico River.

The wind was moaning eerily around the eaves of the
house that night, and after Rick had gone to bed he lay a
long time half awake. In the groan and creak of timbers he
seemed to hear the fierce shouts of pirate crews. And as he
huddled fearfully under the blanket, he imagined that a
dark, bearded face, flanked by great gold earrings, was
staring at him out of the shadows.

Chapter Six

The wind and rain continued next day. At nine in the morning Jed Rowan galloped up the lane on his pony and hailed Rick.

"Get a slicker on an' come quick!" he called. "There's a a boat in trouble in the Sound, an' the Coast Guard's goin' out to help!"

Racing down the road to the harbor front they were in time to see the big motor lifeboat churning out through the channel. She kicked up towers of spray from her bow as she bucked the big waves roaring in from the stormy expanse of Pamlico Sound.

"Too bad we didn't git here in toime to see 'em launch her," said Jed. "They keep the boats in them big boat-houses next to the tower, an' when they run 'em down the ramp, it sho' is a soight."

The boys went into Jack's store to keep dry, and Jed insisted on treating Rick to a Coke. "Oi got some cash," he explained with a grin. "Made it skinnin' toadfish fer Lon Gaskill. They're nasty things to work on, but he pays me seventy-foive cents an hour. Lon gits good money fer the fillets, shippin' 'em to the New York market. Know what they call toadfish up there? Sea squab! Ain't that sump'n? 'Course, they *are* pretty fair eatin'."

Rick was interested. "You suppose I could learn to do

that?" he asked. "I've got to find some way to make a little money."

"Well," said Jed, "Oi reckon you could—if'n you don't moind gittin' yer hands sloimy. There's other jobs, too, loike shuckin' clams an' oysters. An' there's a few folks kin afford to have a boy work 'round their yards. Anything Oi hear about, Oi'll tell you."

More than an hour went by before someone standing outside on the pier yelled that there were boats in sight. The boys hurried out. They could see the lifeboat coming in through the narrow gut, and towing behind it was a yawl, her masts swaying crazily as she rolled in the seas. Twice she bumped on the bar, but the Coast Guard boat kept on pulling. At last they were inside, and in deeper, calmer water. The lifeboat towed the yawl up alongside a long pier, and she was made fast.

"Amateurs, Oi reckon," Jed remarked disdainfully. "Northerners, cruisin' down the Inland Waterway. See that cabin? She prob'ly sleeps four people. Oi bet her keel draws six or seven foot o' water, an' at low toide she'd run on a shoal 'less'n they watched their markers real careful."

The boys hurried over to the Coast Guard station and learned that Jed's guess was correct. The yawl had been blown off course and gone hard aground on the bar, a mile outside the harbor. Scared and shivery, the two men and two women aboard her were taken inside the station for hot coffee.

One of the men who had come ashore from the yawl saw the two youngsters at the door. "Here," he said, "one of you—want to run down to the cabin and bring a couple of blankets to put around these ladies? We got pretty wet."

Rick was off like a flash. He ran along the wharf, jumped down into the sailboat's cockpit, and pulled open the cabin door. The blankets were there, neatly folded at the foot of the bunks. He took two of them in his arms, shut the door again, and scrambled back to the wharf. It was hardly more than two minutes from the time he started till he was back with his load, and only a few drops of rain had fallen on the blankets.

"Good kid!" the northerner exclaimed. "Here—something for your trouble." And he handed Rick a folded dollar bill.

The boy hesitated about taking it. "That's too much," he said. "I just wanted to help."

But the man insisted. "We're all feeling pretty grateful to be safe," he said. "You earned it—go buy yourself something you need. By the way, is there a hotel or some place where we could stay?"

"Sho' is," Jed put in before the Coast Guardsmen could answer. "Oi reckon there's a couple o' rooms at the Wahab Village Hotel. You kin git 'em on the telephone, or Oi could roide over there an' see."

The boatowner laughed. "You Ocracoke lads are mighty obliging," he said. "Thanks. I'll call the Wahab Hotel from here."

Reluctantly the boys departed. "Look," said Rick, "I didn't know he was goin' to give me anything—let alone a whole buck. You take half of it, Jed."

"Not on yer loife!" His friend chuckled. "You earned it, not me. Didn't you say you needed a pair o' swimmin' trunks? They got some fer only a dollar at the Community Store—plain cotton but plenty good enough."

They went together to the store, and Rick proudly carried home a pair of serviceable blue trunks. He wished fervently that the rain would stop. The first thing he meant to do when the sun came out was go swimming in the Sound.

A little before noon, when Rick was eating an early lunch, Jed appeared again. He was on foot this time. "You want to git a good look at the oiland?" he asked. "Rufe

Steele's droivin' his truck up to ketch the twelve-thirty ferry, an' he don't moind havin' comp'ny in the cab. He said he'd take us along, if'n you want to go."

Rick had already split some kindling and filled the wood box. His mother had no objection to his leaving, and he was glad to go. They found Steele's truck pulled up at one of the fishhouses, loading freight.

"Hop in, kids," the trucker told them. "Last few boxes is comin' aboard now."

While they were waiting, Jed explained the operation. "Rufe takes stuff up to the other end o' the oiland, goes across by ferry to Hatt'ras, an' loads it aboard a long-haul truck that takes it north. Then he brings back any freight that moight be there fer Ocracoke."

The burly driver slammed the rear doors and climbed up behind the wheel.

"What you carryin' today, Rufe?" asked the island boy.

"Twenty boxes o' shrimp. Twenty-seven o' mixed fish. Not much of a load. Here—let young Landon set by the winder. You tell him 'bout the oiland as we go."

The truck moved slowly along the village streets, swung to the left past the road leading to the school, and picked up speed as it headed northeastward on the smooth blacktop.

"Yon's the beach," said Jed, pointing off to his right across the sand flats. "An' up ahead, that first dune is First Hammock."

The road ran fairly straight. It was new, built within the year by the state to give Ocracoke Village a route to the northern islands of the Outer Banks. Ahead of them Rick could see occasional dunes, some covered with low-growing trees and bushes. A tidal marsh extended for a long distance on the left, between the road and Pamlico Sound.

"That's Great Swash," said Jed. "Most of it gits flooded at hoigh toide. Good duck-shootin', though."

60

A mile or two farther on he pointed out Quork's Hammock. "Quoite a few spots are named after Ol' Quork," he said. "We done passed Quork's Point, back a ways, an' there's a creek they call Quork's Slew."

"Who was Old Quork?" Rick asked, curious.

It was Rufe Steele who answered. "He lived here a long toime back. Some says he was a poirate. Anyways, he was a half-breed from some place in the West Indies—a real mean cuss that nobody had any use fer. 'Long 'bout the middle o' one March there come a bad storm. 'Twas powerful rough out in the Sound. But Ol' Quork he vowed he'd go out anyhow an' pull his nets. He done blasphemed, they say—'lowed as how the Lord Himself wasn't goin' to stop him. Well, he went out in his boat, all roight, an' that was the last ever seed or heered of him. Ever since then they've called March sixteenth Ol' Quork's Day. Ain't many fishermen willin' to take a boat out that day, 'specially if there's any koind of a storm around."

Jed pointed to the left. "That buildin's the Green Oiland Club," he said. "B'longs to some duck an' geese hunters. They shoot the marsh here, 'round Patch Fench Creek an' Cockrel. Pretty quick we'll be comin' to the Tar Hole Plains. It's jest flat sand, so low a real hoigh toide'll wash clean over this part o' the road."

Several times they had sighted ponies browsing in the marsh grass. Now, as they neared a piece of higher, wooded ground, they saw fifteen or twenty sleek little sorrels and chestnuts among the trees.

Jed chuckled. "They *would* be way up here," he said. "Oi reckon they know Fourth o' July's comin'. Want to make it harder to round 'em up."

"What happens on the Fourth?" Rick asked eagerly. "You mean there's a real roundup, like out West?"

"Sho' there is. Us Scouts roide up here an' droive 'em

down to the village. Soon as they're penned up, the new foals have to be branded. They stay close to their mothers, so it ain't hard to tell who they b'long to."

The road ended at the ferry landing. It was in a little bay, protected from Hatteras Inlet by the hook of sand that formed the upper tip of the island. The ferry was about to pull out.

"Come on, there, Rufe!" yelled one of the deck hands. "Can't wait here all day fer you. Squeeze her in here behind this Buick."

The truck rattled up the ramp, the chain gates were made fast and the rear wheels chocked. The boat held twelve or fifteen cars, packed in four abreast. At the stern on the starboard side was the high pilothouse, and the power came from diesel engines, housed beneath the afterdeck.

"How long does it take to go up to Hatteras?" Rick asked.

"Pretty close to an hour," Rufe Steele told him. "Git out an' stretch yer legs if'n you're a moind."

The boys squeezed out of the narrow space between the cab and the next car and went forward. They were out in the Sound now. Waves hit the square bow of the boat and splashed spray over them, but they didn't mind. A big bird rose from the water ahead and flapped off, twenty yards away. It was like the one Rick had seen earlier.

"Look!" he cried. "Isn't that a pelican?"

"Sho' 'tis," Jed replied unconcernedly. "Lots of 'em 'round here. Cormorants, too, an' gulls, o' course. Look astern, there. Always a mess o' gulls followin' the ferry. Guess they figger folks will be eatin' lunch an' throwin' their leavin's overboard."

There must have been more than a hundred of the noisy birds, white and gray-brown, swirling in the air above the boat's wake. Jed had to shout to make himself heard over their screaming.

The ferry pulled in to the landing at the lower end of

Hatteras Island about one-thirty. There was a huge semi-trailer waiting there to take Steele's boxes of iced fish, and the boys helped pass them down to the men on the ground. After they had unloaded there was time to kill.

"Boat don't go back till three-thirty," said Jed. "Let's go take a look at Hatt'ras Village."

They walked a short distance up the road and came to a few houses. At a small store Jed bought Cokes. " 'Tain't near as pretty here as Ocracoke," he remarked loyally. "Looks sort o' naked to me."

Rick agreed. "I thought there was a big lighthouse at Hatteras," he said, "but I don't see it."

"That's at Cape Hatt'ras," Jed explained, "ten or twelve miles over east o' here. She's big, all roight—tallest on the coast, Oi've heered."

They wandered back to the ferry landing and passed the time until three-thirty listening to the talk between Steele and the crew. Before five o'clock they were back in Ocracoke Village.

*   *   *

It had been the third week in June when the Landons came to the island. As soon as the wind and rain were gone, summer heat settled over Ocracoke. Rick's mother took him out to the back yard one morning and showed him the fig tree, loaded now with green fruit.

"Those figs'll be ripe enough to make preserves in a few more weeks," she told him happily. "My mother taught me the recipe years ago. Wonder if I've still got the knack?"

"I bet you have, Ma," he assured her. "Just say when an' I'll pick 'em for you. Mind if I go over to the Sound an' swim today?"

"Go ahead," she said. "I know it's not deep enough to drown you, but I hope you'll be a little careful."

Rick had never had much chance to learn to swim, but he meant to do it now. Jed and all the other boys he had talked to could swim like ducks. He put on his new trunks and went down the back road, a little self-conscious, hoping not to attract too much attention.

It was too early in the day for the tourists and hotel guests to be swimming, but he saw two local boys already in the water. One was a youngster he had met—Chuck Styron.

"Hoi," Chuck called. "Come on, Rick—she's good an' warm."

Rick waded in up to his waist, then lunged out in an awkward effort to swim. Maybe Chuck thought the water was warm, but it felt pretty chilly to him. He kicked his feet and dog-paddled with his arms, trying to keep his face well above the little waves. Suddenly someone shoved his head under.

When he came up, gasping and choking, the boys were holding their sides with laughter.

"What—wise guy—did that?" he sputtered angrily.

"Oi did," replied a tall black-haired youngster. "No reason to git sore. You cain't learn to swim with yer head held way up. Here's the way to do it."

The boy dove forward and went into a smooth crawl, face down, arms sweeping in slow rhythm, legs stretched out and churning the water behind him. On alternate strokes he turned his head to the left to breathe as he circled the boys and came up beside Rick again.

All Rick's rage was gone in admiration. His grin matched the other boy's. "Okay," he said. "I want to learn to do it like that. Think you could teach me?"

"Whoy not? You got arms an' legs. Here, put yer head down an' hold onto my hands till you git the hang o' the kick."

The lesson went on for twenty minutes, with the other

64

boys giving advice. By the end of that time Rick could keep himself afloat and even swim a few strokes. He thanked the black-haired lad.

"My name's Rick Landon," he said. "Don't believe I've heard yours."

"Oi'm Coley Fulcher. Sort of a fourth or fifth cousin o' yer maw's. 'Tain't often Oi git a chance to teach anybody to swim. All the kids here at Ocracoke learn 'fore they're out o' doi'pers, seems loike."

Rick stayed there another hour, practicing by himself. Now that he knew the fundamentals and had some confidence, swimming seemed a lot easier. The other boys were about to leave, but Chuck Styron saw Rick still in the water and called to him.

"We're goin' out fishin'," he said. "You want to come along?"

Rick accepted without thinking. He ran a little to let the sun dry him off, then hurried after Chuck and Coley. The Styrons, it seemed, had two boats—the big one Chuck's father used to take out fishing parties, and a tubby-looking little fifteen-footer that belonged to the boy himself. The craft was broad-beamed, heavy, and high-sided. It was powered by an ancient two-cylinder inboard engine.

"Oi got only two rods," said Chuck, "but you kin do 'bout as good with a hand loine. Here—you an' Coley kin bait up whoilst Oi git this ol' teakittle agoin'."

Coley sensed that Rick was as unskilled at fishing as he was at swimming. "Here's the clams we'll use fer bait," he said. "Ye do it this-a-way."

Rick stepped into the rocking boat, and it was then that the stale, fishy reek of the bilge water, swashing underfoot, reached his nose. In that moment he remembered how he had felt on the mailboat, and the same uneasiness came to his stomach.

"I—I guess I'd better not go, after all," he stammered.

"Something I was supposed to do for my mother—forgot about it till now."

Coley looked up at his pale face and grinned, beginning to understand. "That's okay," he said. "We'll troy it another toime. 'Tain't rough out there today, though. It's purely ca'm."

Chapter Seven

All the way home Rick was angry at himself. What kind of a landlubber would these kids think he was? Seasick before the boat even left the dock! He'd have to do something to prove to them he wasn't really a coward. And if anybody asked him to go fishing again, he'd do it, no matter how he felt inside.

The mood he was in didn't help matters when he got home. He cuffed little Joey for a fresh remark and was ashamed of his action as soon as he'd done it. The midday dinner Mrs. Landon had prepared was good, but Rick had little appetite for food. He helped sulkily with the dishes, then went out into the little fenced yard. Joey was there, alone, shying pebbles at the trunk of the live oak tree.

"Hey," said Rick, trying to make amends for his earlier bad temper. "How'd you like to go over an' see the ocean?"

Joey's shining face was answer enough. "Gee!" he squealed. "You mean you'd take me?"

"Let's go," his older brother replied gruffly.

Half an hour later they had trudged eastward along the road and across the broad sand flats to the beach. It looked quite different from the shore on the Sound side. Here the big Atlantic breakers were rolling in, crashing on the steep shelf of sand and eddying back in streaks of foam. The air over the surf was alive with birds, and so was the beach itself. Joey wanted to know their names, but Rick had only a vague idea.

"The big ones are gulls," he said. "Two or three different kinds. An' I guess those small ones runnin' on the beach must be sandpipers. There's different kinds o' them, too. Cute little fellers, aren't they?"

Joey nodded, but his interest had strayed to the many-colored shells that were strewn along the sand at the tide line.

"Hey!" he exclaimed. "I'm goin' to start a c'lection! There's millions of different shells. Come on, help me pick 'em up."

For miles the beach stretched away in either direction, and for the moment there was nobody else in sight. In all his life Rick had never been so far removed from people. It gave him a strange feeling of smallness. And yet he was exhilarated, too. This vast beach—all of it—belonged to him and his brother!

For a while he helped Joey collect shells. Then he went back to his birds. Definitely he could distinguish three separate species of gulls. There were the biggest ones, some

white, with black wing tips, yellow bills, and yellow-gray legs; others brownish in color. Then came a group of smaller gulls, more graceful and with a dark tip to their bills. And finally there were the black-headed gulls with cries that sounded like crazy laughter as they swooped down for fish.

Smaller than these, with long, tapered white wings, forked tails, and little black caps on their heads, were birds whose names he didn't know. They soared and sailed above the surf, plunging like arrows when they spotted minnows near the surface.

Rick sat down on the shell-covered crest of sand and watched the busy life of the beach. Hundreds of little

birds, no bigger than the sparrows he had known in Brooklyn, scampered back and forth in the wake of each receding wave. Their sharp beaks probed the wet sand in search of tiny sea animals and shellfish. As he studied them, he realized that they weren't all alike. There were at least four kinds, differing in color, shape, and size. He wanted to know more about them, but he doubted if any of the Ocracoke boys his age could tell him.

At the end of an hour Joey had picked up more shells than his hands and his pockets could hold, and they went back across the sand to the road. A jeep station wagon, with three men in it and half a dozen surf rods in a rack on top, came chugging out to the beach as they left. It had New York license plates. With his lonely paradise spoiled by these intruders, Rick was glad to go home.

Mrs. Landon admired the shells Joey brought into the house. "What about you, Ricky?" she asked. "Aren't you interested in such things?"

He shrugged. "Some o' the shells are pretty enough," he said, "but I like things that are alive. I saw a lot o' birds. You s'pose Mr. Randall would know about 'em?"

"He might. I was on my way over to call on Mrs. Randall. Why don't you come with me?"

The school principal's house was on the south side of Silver Lake, back on a curving road of sand, screened by live oaks, cedars, and yaupon thickets. Outside, it looked like most other houses in the village, a bit dilapidated and weatherworn. But when Mrs. Randall welcomed them in, they found themselves in a cozy sitting room, its wall lined with books.

While the two ladies exchanged local gossip, Rick stole over to one of the bookcases. It wasn't long before he found what he was looking for—a thick volume entitled *Sea and Shore Birds of the Atlantic Coast*. He waited for a pause in

70

the conversation and asked the principal's wife if he might look at it.

"Why, of course you may, Rick," she told him with a smile. "I'm very glad you're interested."

He sat down in a corner and thumbed through the colored plates. The birds he had seen that day, he realized with a thrill, were all here, beautifully pictured. The big white gulls were herring gulls, and the brown ones, he learned, were young birds of the same species. Next he recognized the smaller ring-billed gulls and the black-hooded laughing gulls. The graceful black-capped little fliers were common terns.

It was when he came to the pages of sandpipers and waders that he really grew excited. One by one he identified the different kinds. There were the chunky gray sanderlings and the tiny, trim least sandpipers. Another small bird with a brownish back, short bill, and a little black collar around its throat, he recognized as the ringed plover. On another page he found a beach bird he had seen picking at shells and dead crabs above the tide line. It had a rusty-orange back and a patchy black-and-white head. Its name was the ruddy turnstone.

There was still one he wanted to locate in the book. It was a slim gray wading bird, larger than the sandpipers, with a longer neck, legs, and bill. When it flew, he had noticed a wonderful pattern of dark brown and white on its wings. At last he came to a color plate that showed it both standing and in flight. It went by the somewhat unglamorous name of willet.

"Gee!" he exclaimed, interrupting something his mother was saying. "I'm sorry, Ma, but this book's got everything! You s'pose I could come an' look at it again, Mrs. Randall —when I see some more birds, that is?"

"That's what it's here for," she nodded. "There's a lady

author who comes down here to see the birds, generally in the spring when they're on their way north. I've got one of her books, where she tells about them. If you'd like to read it, I'll lend it to you."

She went to another bookcase, searched a moment, and handed Rick a book. "Take it along when you go," she said. "I'll know where it is if I need it."

He thanked her and looked at the title page. *"Between the Dunes and the Sea,"* he read. "By Rebecca Hamilton." Twenty minutes later, when his mother was ready to start home, she had to call him twice before he heard her.

Mrs. Randall laughed. "It's nice you're so interested," she said. "That's not just a good nature book—it's real literature, beautifully written."

They went out the winding road, past the home of the village nurse. His mother pointed south to the white tower of the lighthouse, looming behind a screen of trees.

"Looks just the way it did when I was a girl," she commented happily. "I do hope you'll learn to like this place, Ricky."

"Oh, I guess it's all right," he admitted. "I like the beach an' the birds anyhow, an' soon as I learn to swim better, I can have more fun."

They were opposite the Styron dock now, and he saw Chuck Styron and Coley Fulcher just climbing out of the old boat. They waved to him.

"Got a noice mess o' fish," Coley called. "They're fluke —more'n we kin eat. You want some, Mis' Landon?"

"If you can spare two or three," she replied, "we'd love them." He brought over three flounder, strung on a piece of old fishline. They were small ones, averaging about a pound apiece. Rick stared at their broad, flat bodies, with both their eyes on one side of the head.

"Know how to fillet 'em?" Coley asked. "Oi could do it fer ye."

"Oh, no," said Mrs. Landon with a laugh. "I remember how all right, an' I'll teach Rick. Next time you go fishing, I hope he can go with you. It's time he learned his way 'round in a boat."

Rick flushed guiltily and gulped. "Yeah," he managed to mumble. "Sorry I couldn't make it today. I'll be seeing you."

*   *   *

Sunday morning dawned hot and fair. As soon as the breakfast dishes were done, Mrs. Landon began getting her sons ready to attend their first Sunday School on the island. First they were thoroughly scrubbed. Then they put on clean underwear and shirts. The weather was too warm for coats, but she insisted that both boys wear neckties and shoes.

It was only a short distance to the church, but they started early, their mother accompanying them. By ten minutes to ten there were fifty or sixty boys and girls waiting outside, along with quite a few older people.

Many of them came up to greet the Landons. One was a Coast Guard officer in a neatly pressed tan uniform.

"My name's O'Neal," he said with a grin. "Reckon you remember me, Annie, from the time we were kids. These your boys?"

She introduced Rick and Joey, and he shook hands with them politely. "I sort o' take charge o' the Cub Scouts," he said, "and it looks like Joey, here, is about the right age to join up. We generally have our meetings Friday evenings, but this week Friday'll be the Fourth o' July, so there won't be one. What do you say—like to join the Cubs?"

"You bet!" piped Joey.

"And this lad," Chief O'Neal went on, turning to Rick, "he ought to be in the Scout troop. I'll speak to Cap'n Howard about it. You'll likely be put in his Sunday School class today, so he'll know who you are."

The church bell began to toll, and everybody started into the white-painted building. Rick and Joey went with the other youngsters to a big room at the rear. When they were settled in their seats, a sun-browned fishing boat skipper prayed in an earnest voice, then called for a hymn. Everybody sang lustily, and the Landon boys joined in.

"Now," said the Sunday School superintendent, "Jed Rowan an' Johnny Garrish'll take up the flower collection."

Rick's mother had told him about that, and he and his brother were prepared. Joey put a penny in the plate and Rick a nickel. One Sunday each month such a collection was taken up, and the money went into a fund to buy flowers if there was a funeral on the island.

The lesson that morning was about the choosing of the twelve apostles. Captain Howard had the boys and girls in Rick's class read aloud from the fourth chapter of the Gospel according to St. Matthew.

"You see," he said, when they had finished, "these men —Peter an' Andrew an' James an' John—they were plain, ordinary fisherfolks like us. Jesus found 'em hauling trawls an' mending nets, alongside the Sea o' Gallilee. He made 'em his full partners—partners in the biggest undertaking the world had ever known up to then—or ever will. An' each one of 'em, with Jesus at the helm, became ten times the man he could ever have been on his own.

"Any time you get discouraged an' think you don't have any chance to amount to much, just remember what the Lord did for those apostles. An' the best part is, He's still ready to do it for us. He's waiting to make us partners, soon as we hear His voice an' follow. You'd be surprised what a man can do if he lets the Lord steer his boat."

The young islanders had listened with rapt attention, and Rick had listened with them. There was a depth of sincerity in the words of the grizzled seafaring man that made him feel an inward wonder. "The way he says it,"

Rick thought soberly, "it sure sounds like something you can believe."

When the lesson was over and another hymn had been sung, the youngsters trooped out into the sunshine. Some joined their parents and stayed for the church service, the Landon boys among them. Their mother didn't believe in doing things by halves.

Joey was a little restless by the time the sermon ended, and Rick's thoughts had strayed to swimming, fishing, and birds, but they all sang the final hymn with gusto. As they made their way out, Captain Howard came over to shake hands.

"Most o' the Scout troop," he told Rick, "will be riding up-island Friday to drive the ponies in. I'm going up with 'em in the jeep. How'd you like to come along?"

"Golly, Cap'n!" The boy beamed. "I'll say I'd like it! Some day do you think maybe I can join the troop?"

"Don't see why not," the captain replied heartily. "We'd be glad to have you. Us Howard kinfolks have got to stick together."

Chapter Eight

That first week of July was a busy one for Rick. He picked nearly two peck baskets of figs and helped his mother with the preserving. The cookstove had to be kept hot throughout the operation, so that he found himself constantly splitting more wood and carrying it in. Strangely enough these chores seemed like fun. Not once was he tempted to grumble about them or to try to beg off from work.

On Thursday, when Chuck Styron came by and invited him to go fishing, his mother urged him to accept. "You've done plenty this morning," she said. "Time you took off for a little pleasure."

Rick wasn't sure how much pleasure it would be, but he had no intention of backing out a second time.

"Okay," he told Chuck with forced heartiness. "Let's go."

The day was fair, with a light westerly breeze blowing in across the Sound. Chuck got the engine going, steered out through the harbor mouth, and turned the wheel over to Rick while he baited up.

"Keep her as she is," he said. "Jest watch the channel markers so we don't run aground. Reckon we'll start with clams fer bait an' see if there's any bottom fish boitin'."

They worked slowly out till they were a mile or two from shore, dragging their lines with the baited hooks a foot from the bottom. Rick got the first bite. It was the first time in his life he had known the thrill of feeling something struggling at the end of a taut line.

"Looks loike he's hooked," said Chuck. "Reel in steady."

He took the long-handled net from the bottom of the boat and sat ready to scoop up the catch. As it came flopping upward, he laughed.

"Jest an old sea robin!" he said. "No good to eat, but we kin use him fer bait."

The fish was a foot long. It had a reddish spot around the gills and big fins that looked like wings. Chuck deftly split it down the back and cut the white flesh into long strips, which he proceeded to put on the hooks. Then they chugged on at two or three miles an hour.

The waves weren't high, but a long ground swell made the boat heave slowly up and down. Rick began to feel uncomfortable in his stomach. He turned so that the other boy couldn't see his face and tried to concentrate on the rod in his hand.

"Ain't seasick, are you?" Chuck asked. "Hit's a moite wamblish out here today."

"Nope," Rick replied through clenched teeth. He was grimly determined that no amount of pitching and rolling was going to make him show his inward turmoil. By luck at that moment he felt a tug on the line and was forced into action. Bud's reel was cranking, too.

"Yippee!" said the island boy. "Mus' be over a school o' fish!"

Two good-sized flounder arrived at the surface at the same time and were swung into the boat. Hastily they were pulled off the hooks and the lines went over the side again. As long as the strips of sea-robin bait lasted, the boys hauled in fish as fast as they could work.

"Whew!" Chuck exclaimed at last, wiping his brow. "Reckon you brung us luck. We got enough to sell at the fishhouse. Must be close to thirty pound here, in all!"

It was queer, but Rick no longer felt the least qualm of seasickness. Even though the ground swell stayed as "wamblish" as ever, he was too busy exulting over their catch to notice. They swung the bow toward home and wallowed along with the wind astern, logging a stout six knots.

At the fish dock, Rick watched proudly as the flounder were weighed in. "Fluke's plentiful roight now," said the man at the scales. "Ain't payin' but twelve cents today. Still an' all, that'll come to some over three bucks."

Chuck insisted on sharing the money equally with his fishing companion. "You earned it," he said, "an' the gas we burned didn't amount to much of anythin'. We'll have to do this again."

Walking home with a dollar-sixty in his pocket, Rick felt like a millionaire. He went whistling into the kitchen and dropped the money on the table with a pleasant jingle.

"Ma," he called, "here's some cash for groceries!"

She hurried in and smiled with surprise as she saw his contribution. "Why, Ricky!" she cried. "You must have caught a lot of fish! I can surely use it, for I had to pay extra haulage on our furniture when it came today. If you'll give me a hand, we can move it right now an' get the place straightened up."

All there had been in the house when they arrived were bare necessities. Now, with their own familiar furniture installed, the rooms began to have a lived-in look. Ricky hadn't really thought of it as home until that moment, but the remembered things settled into the house as if they had always belonged there.

"I guess," he told his mother, "this is goin' to be pretty near as good as Brooklyn after all."

She laughed. "You admit that, do you? Well, one thing it's got that Brooklyn hasn't is a pony roundup on the Fourth o' July. I saw Cap'n Howard today an' he said for you to be ready by seven o'clock tomorrow morning. They're making an early start."

*   *   *

The sunrise sky gave promise of another fine day. It was cool when Rick scrambled out of bed at six, but he knew it would grow hot later on, so he dressed in nothing but a T-shirt and dungarees.

Joey was somewhat jealous because he hadn't been invited by the captain, but he had promised to help his friend Abel decorate his bicycle for the parade. Besides, he would be on hand for the exciting climax of the roundup, when the ponies were driven into the corral.

Rick had finished breakfast and just had time to fill the wood box when Captain Howard drove up in his ancient jeep.

"Most o' the boys set off ahead," he told Rick. "They won't be riding fast, because it's a long way up to the end o' the island. We ought to catch 'em in a mile or two. Hop in an' we'll get started."

The jeep rattled and groaned, but the sturdy little engine kept on chugging. They left the village and went out along the ribbon of blacktop that ran through the sand. Gulls and terns could be seen wheeling above the surf on the right. Even at that distance Rick was proud to think he could distinguish the different species.

As they neared First Hammock, he saw some other good-sized birds flying over the marsh near the Sound. They were black on top, white underneath, and had long bright-red, curving bills. Their cries sounded like the barking of a pack of dogs.

"Cap'n," said Rick eagerly, "what do you call those birds over there?"

The man turned his keen old seaman's eyes to the left. "Them?" he said. "We call 'em black skimmers. Must be

79

hungry, judging by the racket they're making. When the tide's in an' the creeks are flooded, they skim along over the water an' scoop up fish. That's why their lower bill's longer'n the upper one, I guess. When I was a boy, they used to nest in the dunes. Probably still do. Say—aren't those the Scouts, up ahead?"

Through the windshield Rick could see a dozen specks in the distance, moving along in the sand beside the highway. "Yes," he said. "It's funny they don't stay on the road. I should think it'd be smoother."

Captain Howard chuckled. "For a car, yes. But not for ponies. These little Banker horses have never been shod. Their feet aren't accustomed to hard surfaces, but they can go fine in the sand."

"I guess I should have figured that out for myself," said Rick. "Where'd the ponies come from, to start with?"

"Nobody seems to rightly know. Some say they were brought here in Raleigh's ships. Other folks think a Spanish galleon had horses aboard and was wrecked on the reefs off shore. After a couple o' hundred years, the breed naturally got smaller, down to the size they are now. They're smart, though. Had to be, to learn to live on salt grass an' come through storms an' hurricanes. They're kind, gentle little fellows. Make fine polo ponies, an' mighty good riding stock for these island boys."

They drove slowly, in no hurry to overtake the troop. Captain Howard, once started on his favorite subject, told Rick more about the ponies.

"Used to be," he said, "penning 'em was a full-sized job. Must have been more'n three hundred ponies when I was a boy. Some have died, o' course, but a lot have been sold off. Reckon there's only fifty or so, now. But you know, I've seen my father, Homer Howard, bring the whole wild bunch down to the pens singlehanded! He was the best

80

horseman I ever saw anywhere, an' I've done plenty o' traveling.

"My dad used to set off well before dawn, riding White Dandy. That was an Arabian horse my grandfather'd brought from the mainland, and Dad broke an' trained him himself. Fast? He was greased lightning! Father'd be at the head o' the island by daybreak an' start south, driving all the ponies he found ahead of him. Around Tar Hole Plains he'd pick up another bunch. There was a stallion leading 'em, known as Old Wildy—a big, rangy horse with a will of his own. He'd try to make a break an' take his mares back up-island, but he couldn't get away from Dad. The third herd they met up with was near the Great Swash. The stallions would be fighting each other by then an' all the ponies milling around, not wanting to go any further south.

"It was a sight to see Dad handle 'em, all alone. They had to be driven over sand hills an' marshes, through thickets an' across creeks, but he kept 'em moving. The whole sixteen miles he'd make by ten o'clock, an' there wouldn't be a single stray.

"We kids used to climb out on a long live oak limb, where we could get the first glimpse o' the herd coming down toward the village. Weren't any docks in the harbor, those days, an' some o' the ponies would break for the water an' try to swim for it. Folks on foot an' in boats kept 'em headed along the shore toward the big corral. When they were all penned an' the gates closed, everybody'd go home to dinner. Later we'd come back to see the branding an' selling o' the stock.

"My father'd be inside the pen, with a hundred folks sitting on the fence. He'd pick out a wild stallion an' work his way in through the herd, afoot. It had to be done slow an' easy. When he got alongside the stallion, he'd give a

81

sudden jump an' land astride its back. Like a flash he'd grab the mane with his left hand, reach out with his right an' get a grip on the horse's nose, just above the nostrils. Then he had to hang on like a bulldog, for the stallion would rear an' buck an' squall an' paw the air for the next half hour. Finally, when the horse was out o' wind an' so tired he was shaking, he'd give in. I've seen Dad break horses, bareback or under saddle, a lot o' times, an' I never saw him thrown. Mighty few top rodeo riders can claim that much."

Rick had sat enthralled as he listened to this story of other days. "Gee!" he whispered in awe when it was over. "You s'pose we'll see something like that today?"

The captain chuckled. "There'll be some excitement, maybe, but not quite the same. Some o' these Scouts are pretty good riders, an' a bunch o' wild ponies—even fifty of 'em—are bound to give 'em a chance to prove it."

They had come up with the rear rank of the troop now. Jed Rowan, mounted on a handsome little bay mare, gave them a wave of greeting. He was, Rick saw, wearing his Scout uniform and looking very smart. Some of the other boys had dressed up in cowboy outfits or Indian head-dresses in celebration of the Fourth. They yelled and saluted Captain Howard as he drove by. Of the sixteen boys in the group only five were using saddles, though all their mounts wore plain bridles.

"I've noticed," said Rick, "that the Scout ponies are branded with a 'K.' What's that stand for?"

"Well," explained Captain Howard, "a family named Keppel used to own a big bunch of 'em, an' they turned 'em all over to the troop when we formed it. Mighty gener-ous thing to do. We still use the old branding iron on the foals that are dropped by our mares."

He accommodated the speed of the jeep to the trotting of the ponies, leading the way but not moving too far

82

ahead. They had reached the Tar Hole Plains now, and not a single wild horse had been seen.

"Trying to make it tough for us," the captain commented with a grin. "We'll find the whole bunch hiding out in the hammocks yonder would be my guess."

As they approached the dunes, with their crown of low, twisted cedars, Rick caught a glimpse of something moving in the brush. Captain Howard slowed down and waved to the Scouts, gesturing toward the hammock. Up to the northeast, all the way to the ferry landing, there was no other cover that could have concealed a horse.

The troop deployed northward, working around the upper side of the hammock. With whoops and yells they urged their mounts up into the thicket. For a moment the herd could be seen milling around among the trees. Then the ponies broke out, streaming southward along the sand flats, their manes and tails flying.

Rick tried to count them but it was hopeless. They were in too tight a formation and moving too rapidly. His heart beat faster with the excitement of the chase as Captain Howard turned the jeep around and followed the galloping riders.

For two miles the pony herd kept up its furious pace. Then, as they neared the Green Island Club, some of the mares with young foals slowed to a walk. The stallion that led the cavalcade turned back, whinnying and snorting, trying to hurry the stragglers on.

Rick got a good look at him——a handsome brown horse, with a white blaze down his face and a flowing black mane and tail. He pranced nervously as the Scouts approached, then gave one of the mares a warning nip with his teeth and dashed to the front of the herd once more.

"Don't push 'em too fast," Captain Howard shouted. "There's a long way to go yet, an' some o' those little fellows are winded."

The boys reined in their mounts and hung back while the wild bunch moved on at a more leisurely pace. At Quork Hammock half a dozen ponies made a bolt for the brush but were headed off by a watchful pair of riders. For half a mile there was no more trouble. Then suddenly a single young stallion broke out of the herd and dashed away to the right between two dunes. Two mares followed him, with Jed Rowan and Coley Fulcher in hot pursuit.

"He'll swing back up-island, soon as he's hidden by the sand hills!" Captain Howard exclaimed. He gave the wheel a twist and took the jeep jouncing westward through loose sand. Sure enough, as they neared the upper dune, the three runaways come racing toward them. Startled by the car in his path, the stallion reared, his wild eyes rolling and his forefeet pawing the air. For the first time Rick had a good view of him. Smaller than the brown herd leader, this horse was a palomino, so beautiful he took the boy's breath away. His coat was a light, golden tan, his mane and tail the silvery color of corn silk. There was a white star in his forehead.

"Hey!" said the captain. "Where'd that one come from? Don't see any brand on him, do you? An' I don't recall his

being in the roundup last year. He's young, all right. Between a year an' a half an' two years old, I'd say. But what a
colt!"

With another snort the palomino turned and galloped
after the rest of the herd, his mares following obediently.

Jed Rowan's face wore a comical look of chagrin as he
rode alongside the jeep. "They pretty near foxed us," he
told the captain. "Good thing you got over to head 'em off.
Ever see that young stallion before?"

The older man shook his head. "Whoever owns him,
they've got a fine piece o' horseflesh. But it's going to be a
job deciding who the owner is."

"Well, said Jed, "got to git on the job. See you at the
corral." And he and Coley swung their ponies southward
after the moving dust cloud that marked the passage of the
herd.

Chapter Nine

It took nearly three hours to cover the last ten miles to the village. The ponies grew somewhat easier to handle as they went on. And the troop's own mounts were tired enough to enjoy walking instead of trotting. But when they came in sight of the Coast Guard tower, a new restlessness seized the herd. Many of them must have remembered earlier roundups.

The Scouts rode in a wide semicircle at the rear of the procession to prevent any more attempts at escape. Just south of Horse Pen Point they came to the site of an old Navy ammunition dump, where strips of cracked concrete still lay in the barren waste of sand and brush. As soon as they crossed that area, the Scouts let out a whoop and urged the reluctant ponies into a gallop. It was only a minute or two before the herd burst out into the Park Service clearing. Crowds of people had gathered there. They cheered and waved their arms, shooing the ponies away from the Coast Guard station and down to the harbor road.

The brown stallion laid back his ears and led his band at a dead run down the narrow street, lined now by excited men, women, and children.

There was no way for the frightened animals to turn. They raced straight for the open entrance of the corral, in front of Silver Lake Inn. And by the time the hard-riding

86

Scouts caught up with them, every pony in the herd was inside the fence.

"Good work, boys!" Captain Howard called to the troop. "It's getting on for dinnertime, so make sure the gates are tight an' go ahead home. 'Twon't hurt to let these ponies settle down for a couple of hours. Parade starts at two o'clock. I'll see you then."

Rick found his mother and Joey in the crowd and walked home with them. He was so full of the morning's adventure that the words fairly poured out of him. He must have eaten some lunch, but he never could recall afterward what it was.

Joey was having a big day, too. "Wait till you see Abel's bike!" he told his brother. "I bet it'll be the fanciest one in the whole parade! An' guess what—Abel's sister's goin' to be Miss Ocracoke, sittin' on top of a float with a whole mess o' flags. Gee! Fourth o' July was never like this in Brooklyn!"

The parade was to start near the Coast Guard station. By the time the Landons got there, some of the floats were already maneuvering into position and the band was tuning up. Small boys and girls with gaily decorated bicycles were everywhere. Just before two the Scout troop rode up, led by a color guard with Coley Fulcher in the middle, proudly holding aloft the Stars and Stripes.

The Coast Guard had a float shaped like a surfboat, with eight husky men at the oars. There was another one sponsored by the Civic Club, and the largest of all, mounted on a long truck body, was the P.T.A. float. Surrounded by pirates, fishermen, and other island characters, Miss Ocracoke sat on a high throne that was draped with American flags. She was a pretty blond girl of sixteen, dressed in a trim red-white-and-blue bathing suit. Rick whistled appreciatively. He had to admit that young Abel's sister was a knockout.

Everybody in Ocracoke was there by two o'clock. The

band made a couple of false starts, then broke into a loud and spirited Sousa march. The Scouts rode ahead, followed by the floats and a horde of young bicycle riders. And the townspeople fell into step behind them. Past the fishhouses they marched, and the Community Store and the post office. The parade curved around the end of the harbor and brought up in front of the fenced-in area where the ponies were moving about uneasily.

As soon as the column of marchers broke up, everybody hurried to find a vantage point along the fence. Twenty or thirty visitors from off-island were there, and they watched curiously as preparations for the cutting out and branding got under way.

Each horse owner had brought along his own branding iron, hoping to find a foal he could claim. A portable forge had been set up and the coal fire was already hot. Captain Howard climbed high on the fence and waved his hat to attract attention.

"I've asked three Scouts to go in an' single out the young stock," he shouted. "If all you men went in, it'd spook the ponies an' somebody might get tromped or kicked. We'll have the branded mares an' their foals brought over to the fence."

The three boys sent in on the cutting expedition were Chuck Styron, Johnny Garrish, and Jed Rowan. They entered the corral on foot, working their way gently into the herd. Even so, some of the horses and mares took alarm. There was one small stampede, but the Scouts stood still and let the running ponies go past them. When the animals quieted down, Johnny Garrish caught a nursing mare by the forelock and led her slowly toward the fence. A long-legged little filly, not more than three months old, tagged along at her side.

"She's got a Bar-G brand," Johnny announced. "That yours, Mr. Gaskill?"

The owner stepped forward with a delighted grin. "She's ourn, all roight," he answered. "Oi'll hold the little 'un down whoilst you brand her."

The cutting out went on for another twenty minutes, and by that time seven new foals had been claimed and branded, three of them with the Scout troop's "K."

"Oi reckon that's all of 'em," called Chuck Styron, and he started to leave the pen. But Jed Rowan was still moving through the herd. With a quickening beat of his pulse, Rick realized why. His friend was after the unbranded palomino.

In spite of his distinctive color, the colt was doing his best to keep out of sight in the midst of the milling ponies. Jed had a lot of patience. Patting a flank here and offering a bit of sugar there, he worked his way gradually into the center of the close-bunched herd. Twice the colt sensed his approach, snorted, and backed away.

"Come now, baby," the boy was crooning. "We don't aim to do ye any harm. Jest stand easy."

At last he was within arm's length, and the young stallion, shut in by a corner of the fence, had no place to go. Rick clutched the rail and held his breath. This was the moment. He saw Jed tense and crouch, then spring forward, reaching for the silver mane. But the horse was too quick for him. It reared, striking out with sharp fore hoofs, and Jed was lucky to get out of the way. With a sheepish grin he reached the fence and climbed it.

There was an excited buzz of talk among the islanders and tourists. For the first time they had all become aware of the beautiful colt.

"Folks!" boomed Captain Howard in a loud voice. "Listen, everybody! This colt must ha' been missed in last year's roundup. No telling now who his dam belonged to, so the only fair thing to do is auction him off. Who'll make the first bid?"

"Forty dollars!" shouted Steele, the truckman.

"Fifty!" a northern visitor replied.

By five and ten dollar jumps the bidding went up till it reached an even hundred. There it seemed to stop. The auctioneer was about to close it out to the top bidder, a tourist from Baltimore, when another voice was heard. A retired tugboat skipper named Mayhew pointed toward the palomino. "That's the prettiest horse on the island," he called out. "An' I say it ought to stay here. I'll bid a hundred an' twenty-five on behalf o' the Scout troop!"

The whole crowd cheered, and the Maryland man grinned and nodded as he held up his hands in surrender.

"Sold to Mr. Mayhew!" bellowed Captain Howard.

"Now tell us," Mrs. Randall piped up, "who gets the money?"

There was a general laughter. "That's right," called half a dozen voices at once. "If nobody owns him, who's selling him?"

The Park Ranger climbed the fence and waved for attention. He was a lean middle-aged man in a trim green uniform. "You've all heard," he said, when the crowd was silent again, "that the Park Service can't let ponies run loose all over the island now that the new road's built. We're willing to give 'em plenty of acreage, away from the road an' the village, but somebody's got to pay for fencing such an area. I suggest that this money be used to start a fund for it."

It took a moment for the idea to sink in. Then, from one direction and another, the people began to voice their agreement. Mr. Mayhew clinched the matter.

"That's fine," he declared stoutly. "I offered to buy the colt an' I'll pay for him. As I said, I want to give him to Cap'n Howard for the Scouts. You folks get up a committee to take care o' this pony-fencing project an' I'll turn over my check to you."

Captain Howard expressed his pleasure in a little speech

90

of acceptance. "We can sure be proud of a horse as handsome as that," he concluded. "Now all we've got to do is catch him, brand him, an' break him. I reckon it'd be a little too much to ask Mr. Mayhew to do that."

He turned to the nearest group of Scouts. "Who wants to volunteer?"

They looked at one another, grinned, and hung back. Even Jed didn't offer to attempt it again. But some crazy impulse made Rick step forward.

"I—" he croaked with a dry throat, "I'd like to try."

The faces around him showed everything from amazement to open derision. A lanky towheaded Scout, a year older than Rick, pointed at him and slapped his thigh.

"Him!" He guffawed. "Who ever heard o' bustin' broncs in Brooklyn? Hey, guys, this sure oughta be a treat!"

Jed Rowan scowled. "Oi'll help ye, Rick," he said quietly, "if ye really want to go through with it."

Rick had turned pale and his knees were trembling. He wondered what on earth had gotten into him, but there was no turning back now.

Captain Howard gave him a pat on the shoulder that steadied him. "Just keep the colt in that corner where he is now," he advised Rick in a low voice. "Back him up so his tail's against the fence. Once we get a hold of it we can hang onto him."

With some of the other Scouts, Captain Howard hurried around outside the corral. Rick and Jed climbed in and began their wary approach to the palomino. He had stayed where Jed had left him, five or six feet from the fence corner. As the boys came nearer, he pawed the ground and tossed his head, then backed away from them a step at a time. Rick saw the long tail flick against the rails. The captain reached in, seized it with both hands, and pulled back till he could wrap it around a post.

"Got him!" he called. "Stand clear till he quiets a bit!"

The young horse squealed and reared but was unable to free himself. Rick felt calmer now. He began to remember some of the things he had seen the riders do at Madison Square Garden when they were readying a wild mustang to get him into the chute.

"Look," he told Jed, "we've got to get a rope on him an' blindfold his eyes 'fore we can even get close with a saddle —or a branding iron either."

"Oi'll fetch a rope," Jed replied, and hurried off.

Rick stood in front of the colt and tried to plan what he would do. It was only a minute till Jed returned. He not only had a thirty-foot length of rope but a torn shirt that could be used as a blindfold.

Rick made a running noose in one end of the rope. It wasn't too expert a job, but he thought it would serve. Then he moved up quietly on the palomino's flank.

The stallion was still rearing and plunging, but his tail was held by a double turn around the post. Rick didn't try to spin the loop. He simply shook it out till it was three or four feet across, drew it back, and flung it high over the horse's head, hoping and praying his aim was true. The noose settled around the arching neck, and the onlookers let out a cheer.

"Quick, Jed!" Rick panted. "Gimme a hand!"

Together they pulled the rope tight and hung on while the colt reared in frantic terror. With his wind partially cut off by the noose, he finally stood gasping, all four feet planted on the ground. Rick passed the free end of the rope through the fence and took a double half hitch around a post, pulling the palomino's head down.

"That's it, boys," the captain called. "You've got him moored fore an' aft. Long as he stands still he won't choke to death."

Slowly and gently, Rick tied the old shirt over the pony's

eyes. "All right," he told his companion wearily. "I guess we can brand him now."

The iron had been kept hot. Jed took it as it was passed between the rails, braced himself, and planted the smoking "K" squarely on the sweaty golden flank. The colt didn't kick or thrash about. He just stood shuddering as the hot iron seared the hide. And Rick shuddered with him.

"It don't hurt fer more'n a minute," Jed said reassuringly. "If we untoied him now, he'd be frisky as ever. But first we gotta git a saddle an' bridle on him an' see if one of us kin roide him. Oi wouldn't want to try it with all these other ponies in here."

Captain Howard had already thought of that. He sent half a dozen mounted Scouts into the corral, and in a matter of minutes the herd had been driven out, while the crowd scattered in haste. Soon the ponies, led by the brown stallion, were pounding away up the island.

Someone handed a saddle and bridle over the fence. With the blindfold still in place, Jed was able to get the bit between the colt's teeth and buckle the cheek strap. The saddle blanket went on the quivering back, then the saddle. Both boys pulled on the broad bellyband and cinched it tight.

Jed checked the length of the stirrups. "It's moy saddle," he said, "an' the stirrups fit me okay. Oi reckon we got about the same length legs. Le'me have a go at it if you don't want to."

Rick shook his head. "I'm goin' to try," he said with a wan grin. "But I never rode a horse before, so you'd better be ready to pick up the pieces."

Chapter Ten

Most of the spectators had come back when Rick let go of
the fence and settled himself in the saddle. He knew his
mother must be there somewhere, but he was afraid to look.
He got both bare feet in the stirrups and gripped the reins
in his left hand.

"All right," he told Jed through clenched teeth. "Let
him go."

The other boy snatched the blindfold off and released
the rope. Captain Howard had loosed the tail at the same
time. For two or three seconds the palomino stood there,
head up, breathing deep. Then he realized he was free. He
gave one tremendous lunge out into the middle of the corral, put his head down, and began to buck.

Rick hung on. One spine-jarring jolt followed another,
but he managed to land back in the saddle each time. Then
the young horse sunfished, twisting in the air till his rider
was dizzy. Both feet had lost the stirrups now, and Rick
knew his luck had about run out. Still he refused to grab
for the pommel. Waving his right arm like the rodeo riders
and kicking the colt's sides with his heels, he waited for the
inevitable instant when he would be thrown clear. He had
tried, anyhow.

Suddenly the bucking stopped. The palomino started to
run. Round and round the pen they flew, skidding at the

turns. Rick's breath was gone, but he succeeded in finding the stirrups again and was able to haul back on the reins. The pony's mouth was tender, and though the bit was only a plain bar affair, the pressure told. Gradually the furious pace slowed to a trot, then a walk.

Hardly believing he was still alive, Rick guided the young horse over to the fence and swung stiffly down from the saddle. He handed the reins to Jed and leaned his head against the rails, too dazed for the moment to know that people were cheering all around him.

It was Captain Howard who brought him back to his full senses. He felt a powerful clap on his back and heard the old mariner's hearty voice. "Boy," the captain was saying, "you did it! Best ride I've seen since I was a youngster!"

He led Rick over to the colt. "Here," he said, "give him a piece o' this apple. Let him know you're his friend after all."

The palomino shied a little at Rick's approach, but the boy patted his neck and held out half an apple. At last the tempting scent of it overcame the colt's fear. He fumbled for it with velvet lips, took it, and munched daintily. The saddle and bridle were still on him.

"Take a ride, Jed," Rick urged. "See if he wants to do any more tricks."

He held the bridle while the island boy mounted. This time there was no trouble. At the touch of Jed's heels the young horse trotted amiably around the corral while the crowd applauded. Rick watched with a glow of pleasure. The palomino was almost as beautiful under saddle as he had been on the open range. And it was he—Rick Landon —who had tamed him.

*   *   *

Troop 290 held a special meeting before supper that evening and took Rick in as a Second Class Scout. Jed told him about it later, on their way to the square dance.

96

"We voted to let you skip Tenderfoot," he explained. "Reckon most everybody figgered you'd proved you were fitten to be a reg'lar Scout, long as most o' what we do is roide. O' course, you'll still have to study up in the Handbook, learn the Scout Law an' all that. Oi'll lend you moine till you kin git one o' your own."

The recreation hall back of the schoolhouse had been specially decorated for the holiday. Crepe-paper streamers in the national colors festooned the walls and ceiling. Already, when the boys arrived, there were seventy or eighty people in the hall, and at least half of them were teen-agers like themselves. In one corner Rick heard a scraping of strings as the musicians tuned up. There were two fiddles, a guitar, and an accordion—just right, Jed said, for country music.

Across the floor Rick saw the tall towhead who had made fun of his offer to ride the wild colt. He was dressed up now in a fancy sport shirt and talking to Sally Dennis—the Miss Ocracoke of the parade.

"Who's that guy?" Rick whispered. "Friend o' yours?"

Jed grinned. "Not roightly a friend," he said. "Name's Wesley Jenkins, but we all call him Windy. His ol' man's a guide fer off-island folks that come fer the huntin' an' fishin'. They moved here a couple o' years back, from some place on the mainland—Beaufort, seems loike. Windy don't git on too good with the rest o' the Scouts."

Rick said nothing, but he thought he understood why. At that moment Mr. Randall came over to greet them.

"How are you, Jed?" he asked. "And you, Rick? Seems to me you made quite a name for yourself today. That was a fine, plucky ride. Congratulations!"

The school principal was the first of many—grownups and youngsters alike—who came up to compliment him. But the praise didn't turn his head. He knew better than anyone else how near he had been to defeat. "I was just plain lucky," he told his well-wishers, his face growing redder by the minute. "Any o' the other boys could have done it better."

Fortunately, the music soon struck up and sets began to form on the floor. "Choose yer partners!" yelled the caller. "All set fer Birdie in the Cage!"

It was the first square dance the Brooklyn boy had seen. A week earlier he would probably have called it "corny," but something had happened that wiped out most of his prejudices. Before long his feet were tapping in time to the lively tunes.

When the first figure ended, he saw Coley Fulcher coming toward him, pulling a girl by the arm. She was a year or so younger than Coley, but she looked like him—the same long legs and dark hair and sparkling eyes.

"This here's my sister, Rick," said Coley with a grin. "Name's Judy Ann. Oi reckon she'd be proud to dance with you, only she's too bashful to say so."

"I—I never tried it," Rick stammered. "It's nice to meet you, Judy Ann, but I'm 'fraid I can't dance."

"Shucks!" Coley laughed. "Never rode a buckin' horse, either, did you? But you made out good enough. Come on —we'll all be in the same set, an' you'll learn quick."

"Partners up an' make yer circle," shouted the caller, and he began to clap his hands and tap his foot. Rick, with Judy Ann clinging to his arm, found himself in a group with three other young couples.

"Balance off!" sang the caller. Then, "All hands 'round . . . circle to the left an' keep in step!"

The fiddlers beat out the time and it was easy to fall into a quick, rhythmic shuffle that seemed to go with the music. Rick's left hand was held by Judy Ann, his right by another girl—the one Coley had picked.

"Back to the roight an' hol' on toight!" came the call. Then, "Dosie-doe an' alleman' left!"

"Expertly, Judy Ann helped him through the maneuver. Before he had time to fumble, he had gone behind her, back to back, and was moving around the circle in a right and left weave that brought him back to his partner again.

"Swing yer gal with a roight-han' swing!"

Laughing, he swung her as the rest were doing and found her amazingly light on her feet. The calling went on. All he had to do, he discovered, was watch the others and follow their lead, matching his step with Judy Ann's twinkling feet. It was easier than he had expected, and it was fun.

The figure ended with a "Promenade all!" and the dancers, flushed and panting, went over to the refreshment table for Cokes and cookies.

"Gee," said Rick, as they sipped their drinks. "You're sure good at it, Judy Ann. Sorry I was so clumsy. S'pose you could show me that 'dosie-doe' thing again? If you aren't afraid o' getting stepped on, I'd like to dance the next one with you, too."

She dimpled shyly. "I'd jus' be delighted, Rick," she replied. "I saw you ride that horse an' I thought you were wonderful. What do you think you'll name him?"

"Name him? Me? Why, he belongs to the troop, an' I guess they'll decide. What would you call him?"

Judy Ann blushed. "I thought," she murmured, "because he's yellow an' all, his name might be Dandelion."

"Hey, that's good!" he said. "I'll suggest it to Cap'n Howard. Listen, the music's starting up. Want to get into a set?"

Two or three groups of youngsters had already formed up. Rick and Judy had to join a set with some older people, but they found it as much fun as ever. Chief Ben O'Neal and his wife went through the figures with all the snap of teen-agers and a lot more skill.

By the time the dancing ended, at ten-thirty, Rick

had learned enough to feel at home on the floor. He walked Judy Ann Fulcher home, in company with several other young couples. There was a moon, and mockingbirds were singing in the soft Carolina night. On the way back to his own house he stopped a minute to listen. Then he stretched his muscles, tired from the dancing and stiff from the ride, and grinned to himself. He was happier than he had ever been in his life.

*   *   *

The next day, Saturday, the Ocracoke Scout troop had plenty to do. The corral fence had to be taken down and the posts and rails stored until next year. With twenty boys and men at work, the job was finished by noonday. Then Rick went with Captain Howard to visit the colt, which had been kept overnight in his stable.

"Reckon he ought to have a name," said the captain. "After paying all that money for him, I thought Mr. Mayhew should have the say about that, but he left it up to us. You got any good ideas?"

"Well," said Rick, "I was sort o' thinking we might call him Dandelion. I bet he's got some of old White Dandy's blood in him—the one your father used to ride. An' then, when the sun hits that yellow coat o' his—well, it seems as if Dandelion fits him."

To his delight, Captain Howard agreed at once. "You may be right about the colt's blood lines," he said. "A white Arab, crossed with a chestnut mare, might give you a color like this after a few generations. He's sure built like old Dandy, too, only a size smaller. So Dandelion it is!"

The captain showed Rick how to use a currycomb and brush. It was a pleasure to see how the golden hide responded to a little work, and the young stallion, after some nervousness at first, seemed to enjoy the feel of it.

"He needs to be ridden, too," Captain Howard commented. "Put this saddle on him an' see how he acts today."

The saddle went on without trouble, but when Rick tried to put the bit in the colt's mouth, he encountered some difficulty. Dandelion bobbed his handsome head and pulled away.

"Pat him a bit," advised the captain. "Then get your right arm over his head an' hold the bridle in your left."

Rick stroked the stallion's sleek neck softly, gradually working his arm upward till the crook of his elbow held the head down. Little by little he pushed the bit between lips and teeth, drew the top of the bridle over the ears, and buckled it fast. Then, with the reins in his hand, he put his left foot in the stirrup and swung his right leg over the cantle.

The pony quivered for a moment, and Rick wondered if he was about to buck. But when he spoke to him gently and touched his side with a bare heel, Dandelion moved smoothly forward and trotted out the driveway to the road. Rick wasn't conscious of guiding his mount in the direction of the Fulchers' house, but that was where he found himself a few minutes later.

Judy Ann came running out on the porch. "Hi!" she called gaily. "My, but he looks wonderful! You must have used furniture polish on him."

Rick chuckled. "Just elbow grease. Guess what his name is," he said teasingly. "That's right—Dandelion! Captain Howard thought it was just the name for him."

The colt grew restless before they could talk longer. Rick waved good-by and rode out to the sand flats above the village. There he let the pony out. For five minutes they galloped northeastward at a pace that took Rick's breath away. Then he reined the colt in and rode him back. He stopped at his own home.

"Hey, Ma," he called. "Come have a look!"

She came outside, her expression a mixture of pride and

worry. "Isn't he beautiful!" she said. "But I declare—for a city boy you do take a lot o' chances with your neck. Has he been trying to buck you off again?"

"No," Rick said with a laugh, "he's gentle as a kitten. Have you got an apple handy? He deserves a treat."

When she brought it, he broke the apple in two. "You give it to him," he said. "He won't bite you."

She held the fruit out timidly, and Dandelion took it in his soft mouse-colored lips, winning her heart at once. "Oh, you lovely thing!" she exclaimed. "And to think how you acted up yesterday! Are you going to ride him all the time, Rick, now that you're in the Scouts?"

"Guess not," he told her regretfully. "He belongs to the troop. But I'm sure I'll get to ride him some o' the time."

When he took the colt back to the Howard stable, the captain told him to turn the palomino loose.

"His stomach isn't used to regular horse feed," the older man explained. "All his life he's lived on salt grass an' water he digs out o' the sand with his hoofs. Any time you boys need him, you'll be able to catch him. He's got to know you now, an' I don't believe he'll put up much of a fuss."

Rick took the saddle off, then the bridle. He gave the young stallion a slap on the flank. For a moment Dandelion stood, head high, ears pricked toward the north. Then he was away with a quick scurry of hoofs. Two or three minutes later they heard his glad neigh of freedom, somewhere off in the dunes.

Chapter Eleven

Now that he was a member of the Boy Scouts, Rick saw more of the island youngters. He had already developed a strong friendship with Jed Rowan and Coley Fulcher, but there were other boys he liked and admired. He went fishing with Chuck Styron and Johnny Garrish and hiked along the beach and over the dunes with Barney O'Neal. Barney was sixteen and ready to start his senior year in school the next fall. He was tall and strong, probably the best athlete in Ocracoke. But in addition to swimming, riding, and playing baseball, he liked to read books on any scientific subject.

Rick discovered that Barney knew more about birds than any of his other friends. That was one reason why they explored the island together. The older boy showed Rick his first royal tern—a bird marked much like a common tern, but nearly as large as a laughing gull. On another expedition into the dunes they found a hollow in the sand with four eggs in it. These were quite a bit smaller than hen's eggs, and a pale bluish color, mottled with dark brown spots.

"Don't touch 'em," Barney warned. "If we beat it out o' here quick enough, maybe the mother bird'll come back, an' we can foind out what sort she is."

They went thirty yards away on the other side of the dune

and settled down to wait. Within a minute or two, a black-and-white bird flew rapidly in from the tide-covered flats. Her long red beak opened as she approached the nest, and she let out the harsh, barking cry that Rick had heard before.

"Black skimmer!" he said.

"Roight," Barney replied. "Watch out—here she comes!"

They ducked their heads as the angry bird swooped like a whirlwind to within a yard of them. The attack continued until they turned tail and scurried off in haste.

Barney laughed. "Real mad, wasn't she? Ever seen skimmers when they're fishin'? Come on; let's go over by the marsh an' watch 'em."

There must have been fifty of the graceful birds soaring over the shallow water. Every few seconds one would glide downward, dip its lower bill just under the surface, and fly along, leaving a V-shaped ripple behind. A moment later the bird would climb, turn, and come back over the same course, snapping up the tiny fish that had been lured to the top of the water.

"Their roight name's Rynchops. Greek or Latin, Oi guess. Miss Hamilton told me about 'em when she was here last spring."

"Gee," Rick replied in awe, "you mean the lady author? I sure hope she comes back an' I can meet her. Mrs. Randall loaned me a book she wrote."

"You'll loike her," Barney told him. "She's real folksy. Don't moind a bit talkin' to kids that are interested in birds an' such."

They crossed back to the ocean side of the island and worked northeastward, leaving the surf fishermen far behind. On a lonely stretch of beach Barney suddenly caught Rick's arm and stopped. He was pointing to a distant group of gulls near the edge of the water.

"Come on," he said in a low voice. "Let's git closer to

104

'em. Oi've got a hunch them two biggest ones moight be great blackbacks!"

They moved slowly, trying not to alarm the flock. Most of them, Rick could see, were herring gulls. But two birds towered above the rest. They had huge white heads and massive yellow bills. And their backs and wing covers weren't gray, like the other gulls', but glossy black.

"Golly!" Barney whispered. "Ain't they a soight? Big as turkeys! They don't git this fur down the coast very often. Matter o' fact, Oi've only seen 'em once before in moy loife."

The boys watched for half an hour, then turned back regretfully, for it was nearing suppertime. Farther down the beach, they found some excitement among the surf-casters. A wealthy fisherman from New Jersey had just landed an enormous drumfish, and the others had gathered to look it over.

"Bet he'll weigh sixty pounds!" one exclaimed. "That ought to win you some kind of a prize, Charlie."

"What do you mean—sixty pounds?" the lucky angler retorted. "He'll go seventy-five or better!"

Barney was laughing as they walked away. "Wait till he gits him on the scales," he said. "It was a noice big drum, roight enough, but it won' run more'n fifty-foive pound. Ferd Gaskill got one that big last week."

*　　　*　　　*

On half a dozen occasions that summer the Scouts went for troop rides. Rick was a full-fledged member of the organization now. He had studied the Handbook, passed his first tests, and been formally inducted. While he had no uniform as yet, he saved every penny he could earn in order to buy one.

From the other boys he learned more about Captain

Howard, the remarkable man who had organized the island troop four years earlier.

"He's led a real active loife," Jed Rowan told Rick as they rode over the dunes. "Went to sea when he was eighteen or so, an' in World War I he was a gunner's mate on a destroyer. Afterwards, he got in the Army Engineers an' worked on sea-goin' dredges fer a good many years. By the toime World War II come along, he was a lieutenant colonel an' sailed in command of a whole fleet of cargo ships an' dredges that went to Europe to clean out navigational hazards ahead o' the big invasion. Then, after the war, he did some more dredgin', workin' all over—in Mexico an' Venezuela an' California.

"When he come home to Ocracoke to retire, he didn't want to jest set around, so he started the Scouts. Hit's sho' been a foine thing fer us kids."

"He's been mighty good to me," said Rick soberly. "The one thing I wanted most, when I lived back in the city, was to ride horses. If it hadn't been for Cap'n Howard, I guess I'd never have made it."

He was on Dandelion that day. He lifted the reins, clucked to the palomino, and away they flew over the sand.

Finding things to do to earn money had been easier than Rick expected. He was a fairly good swimmer now, and several times he got jobs baby-sitting at the Sound-front beach, while tourist parents were out fishing. The going rate was fifty cents an hour, and he sometimes put in three or four hours at a stretch. Most of his other jobs were harder and dirtier—hauling sand, for instance.

The crest of the ocean beach, where Joey had found his shells, contained a type of sand that made good mortar. When an occasional house was built that summer, Johnny Garrish would use his father's old pickup truck to get sand from the beach for the foundations. Twice he hired

106

Rick to help him do the shoveling. The only way they could cross the soft sand with a load was to let some of the air out of the tires, giving the truck more traction. And even then Rick had to push from behind when the wheels began to spin. He really worked for the two dollars Johnny paid him.

Skinning toadfish at the dock wasn't as hard a job physically, but at first he thought it even more unpleasant. The fish themselves were repulsive, and there was a knack to skinning them that took him several days to learn. Meanwhile, he was up to his elbows in blood and slime and came home at night smelling so fishy that his mother wouldn't let him in the house. What he did was leave his dungarees in the back yard, slip into his trunks, and go for a swim in the Sound before supper.

The skinning was piecework, paid by the pound of cleaned fish. At first he was lucky to make a dollar a day, but he stuck to it till he was almost as fast as Jed Rowan. Then, just as he got up to three dollars, the run of toadfish petered out.

Between such jobs, Rick had some work to do around home. There was no wood box to be filled, for Mrs. Landon had ordered a supply of coal as soon as she got part-time employment clerking at one of the stores. The coal was stored in a shed behind the house, and a bucketful had to be carried in each morning. There was also a small vegetable garden that must be weeded and hoed.

By the middle of August, Rick had saved up a total of fourteen dollars. His mother borrowed a mail-order catalog from Uncle Dan Howard, and together they filled out the order form for an official Boy Scout uniform. It came two weeks later, in time for the Labor Day Jamboree.

The jamboree was an event dreamed up by the troop in an effort to raise more money for the pony fencing. There

107

would be a good many tourists and visitors on the island that weekend, and the Scouts all worked hard to put together an entertainment worth paying to see.

Their plans started with the simple idea of some trick riding—cowboy and Cossack stunts such as they had seen in the movies or on television. Then somebody suggested a musical ride, like the ones staged by the Royal Canadian Mounted Police. There was some doubt whether their ponies could be trained to trot or canter to the perfect time required, or to maneuver in twos, threes, fours, and line abreast.

While they were discussing it, Rick came up with a new idea. He had been a regular attender at the weekly village square dances and knew that every boy in the troop was familiar with the figures. Why not, he suggested, have a mounted square dance?

Some were skeptical, but Coley and Jed backed him up enthusiastically. "We've got the music—the same fellers that play in the recreation hall," said Jed. "An' those ponies kin turn on a doime. Oi bet they'd have fun doin' it. All we'd need is plenty o' practice beforehand so we could make up one good set."

After some further talk, the troop agreed to try it. Next morning they rounded up some twenty ponies and started rehearsing out on the sand flats near First Hammock. They chose that spot because they didn't want the townspeople to get any advance hint of what they meant to do.

For music they had a harmonica, played by Coley's young brother Ronnie. The boy had a good sense of rhythm, and he could play half a dozen square dance tunes, such as "Turkey in the Straw" and "Skip to My Lou."

Captain Howard did the calling. For the first few days they had two sets of eight riders each, and they stuck to the simplest figures. As Jed had foreseen, the ponies enjoyed
108

it. They made their turns obediently and quickly. Sometimes it almost seemed as if they kept step to the jigging music.

But there were wide differences in the ability of the riders. The captain experimented with various pairs, trying to get boys who worked well together. Finally, on the Saturday before Labor Day, he cut the original group to eight.

"Folks can't very well watch two sets at once," he said. "It'd be like a two-ring circus. So I aim to pick the best riders an' the best-trained ponies. Don't take it hard if you're left out."

The first seven boiled down to Barney O'Neal, Coley Fulcher, Jed Rowan, Chuck Styron, Johnny Garrish, and a couple of other boys who were good riders but not close friends of Rick's. The final choice lay between Windy Jenkins and Rick, himself. Two or three times they went through the most complicated of their figures, taking turns as partners of Coley Fulcher.

Rick, riding Dandelion, did the best he knew. Wes was on a raw-boned sorrel horse, less graceful than the palomino but equally quick. After the last "Promenade all!" the captain made his decision.

"Near as I can see," he said, "you both do all right. But that colt, Dandelion, is too pretty to leave out. Folks that saw him broke'll want to see him again, an' Rick's the one that knows him best. Sorry, Wesley, but that's the way it'll have to be."

Jenkins wasn't a good loser. "Okay," he said with a scowl, "see if I care. Everybody knows this Landon kid's a pet o' yours."

"Listen, boy," said the captain coldly. "Let's get this straight. I've had to handle men an' make decisions all my life, an' I've never played favorites. I think you owe me an apology."

"Aw, I didn't mean nothin'," Windy mumbled, and the incident appeared to be closed.

Rick had been keeping the palomino tied up in the back yard. That night he rode home with an uneasy feeling. Twice, before bedtime, he went out to make sure the colt was all right. The first time, Dandelion whinnied softly at his approach, and he fed him an apple. The second time the young horse was lying down, sleeping peacefully.

*   *   *

By Sunday morning the full tide of visitors had arrived, and the hotels and tourist lodges were full to capacity. Every seat in the church was taken that morning. Outside, when the service was over, Rick looked proudly at the homemade posters advertising the jamboree. He heard some of the older people talking about it.

"The boys say they got a real surproise fer us," one man was telling an off-island guest. "Won't say what, but the way they kin roide them ponies, Oi've got a hunch it'll be worth watchin'."

The Park Ranger had agreed to let them use the area near the Coast Guard station for their show. It was level ground, and there were enough benches to accommodate a hundred or more spectators. Monday morning all the preparations had been made. The Scouts rode out of town early that afternoon to give their mounts a bit of exercise, then returned and got into their uniforms. The jamboree was scheduled to start at three-thirty.

The committee to raise funds for the fencing had taken over the job of selling tickets and recruited some of the island's prettiest girls to handle them. When Rick rode down to the Park Service area, he found Sally Dennis, Judy Ann Fulcher, and several others standing in little booths at the entrance. Already they were doing a land-office busi-

110

ness. Natives and visitors alike were glad to support a good cause.

The regular square-dance band, augmented by a cornet and a trombone, had arrived early, and their gay music helped to pass the time for the steadily growing crowd. Rick began to have butterflies in his stomach. From the actions of his friends he could tell that the other riders felt the same way he did, and some of their nervousness communicated itself to their mounts. The ponies tossed their heads and pawed restlessly at the sand.

At the appointed time, Captain Howard climbed up on one of the picnic tables. He called for order in his deepest quarterdeck voice.

"You folks are here," he said, "to help us keep our herd o' Banker ponies. They're one o' the sights that have made Ocracoke famous, an' the National Park Service doesn't want us to lose 'em."

He went on to give a brief history of the ponies and describe the need for a fenced range.

"The Boy Scouts have worked hard to give you a show you'll enjoy," he concluded, "an' I think you're going to like it. To start things off, we'll have some trick bareback riding "

As he got down, the band blared out a fanfare, and little Andy Richards rode into the open space. Andy was only twelve, the smallest boy in the troop, but wiry and agile as a monkey. He was on a clever, fleet-footed little chestnut mare. First he circled the arena twice at breakneck speed. Then he dropped a handkerchief, rode off a hundred yards, and dashed back, leaning far over to pick it up at full gallop. After that, he climaxed his solo exhibition by going completely under the mare's neck and up the other side, still on the run.

Before the applause died down, two other Scouts rode

out to join him. With the ponies trotting three abreast, the boys stood up on their backs and made a round of the cleared space. Then little Andy climbed nimbly to the shoulders of the other two, balancing with arms outspread as he formed the top of a pyramid.

It was beautifully done. While the crowd roared its appreciation, Rick and the other square dancers looked on with dry throats, hoping their performance would be half as good.

"Thanks, boys, that was fine," Captain Howard boomed out. "An' now we're coming to the main event—the treat o' the day—that we've managed to keep pretty much a secret up to now. Let's have a little music, you fellows in the band!"

Chapter Twelve

During the first part of the show, the eight Scouts in the square dance set had dismounted and moved close to the arena to watch the trick riding. Now they hurried back to their ponies. The four who were to take the parts of girls put on big sunbonnets and tied frilly aprons around their waists. While he was adjusting his apron, Rick suddenly noticed that Dandelion was acting more fidgety than the other horses. The colt snorted, tossed his head violently, and shook himself like a dog coming out of water.

"Hey—what's the trouble, Dandy?" the boy asked anxiously. He tried to stroke the young stallion's neck, only to have him jerk away and rear a little.

"Wait for me, guys!" Rick panted. "There's something wrong! Here, Jed, hold his head while I try the girth."

When he hauled tighter on the cinch, the palomino squealed as if in pain and pulled back against the bridle reins.

"It don't seem loike colic," said Jed. "Quick! Git the saddle off an' see if somethin's botherin' him. Could be a wasp or a bee."

Rick snatched away the saddle and lifted the pad. Under it, firmly imbedded in the felt, was a big sandspur.

"Gosh!" Jed groaned. "No wonder the poor cuss was mommicked! Them spoikes was prickin' clean through his hoide. How the heck did it git there?"

Rick soothed the pony down before he spoke. Then he put back the pad, turning it the other way up, and cinched the saddle.

"Somebody did it on purpose," he said grimly. "I don't know who, but if I ever find out, I'll make him wish he hadn't."

By this time the musicians had played through two choruses of "Old Zip Coon," and the spectators had begun craning their necks to see what was holding things up.

"You all set at last?" Coley Fulcher asked. "Come on, then—let's git in our places!"

They rode out in pairs to the call of "Partners up!" and trotted around in a circle in time with the jigging tune.

"First couple out—give the lady a twirl!"

Barney O'Neal bowed to his partner, Jed, then grabbed his hand, and their ponies made a tight swing around each other while the crowd laughed and cheered. Each couple followed suit. Then there was a *dos à dos,* or "dosie-doe" as Rick knew it, and a grand right and left. By that time both boys and ponies were in the swing of it, and they moved through the whole figure without mishap, spinning their partners at the end in a flurry of pink and blue sunbonnets.

There was a short intermission for soda pop before they tackled another figure, and another. The windup was the toughest of the lot—"Birdie in the Cage." Once a pony stumbled and unhorsed its rider, but the boy was up again in a flash and they came through in a blaze of glory. When it was all over, they received a tremendous hand from the onlookers.

Quite a few of the off-island people had been taking pictures during the performance, and Chief O'Neal of the Coast Guard had filmed the whole affair with a movie camera.

"I don't know how good the film'll be," Rick heard him

114

telling Captain Howard. "But if it turns out well, we might use it to get some publicity on the mainland—raise more money for the fencing."

"Good enough!" said the older man. "Let's run it at the next Scout meeting an' see how it looks."

He turned to Rick. "That was a mighty fine idea of yours for the square dancing," he said. "Went off well, too. But I was commencing to get worried, there at the start. What held you boys up?"

Rick told him about the sandspur under the saddlecloth. "Didn't seem possible it could get there by accident," he added. "It looked to me as if somebody wanted to see Dandelion do some fancy bucking."

Financially, the jamboree had been a success. Rick heard next day that they had taken in more than a hundred dollars. The pony-fencing fund was growing.

School would be starting later in the week, and Rick had been dreading it. To him the very word "school" had a dreary sound. It had always meant confinement in a dingy building, poorly lighted and ventilated, like the one that had housed P.S. 68. Worse still, it meant reciting to teachers who had little interest in their jobs and who put most of their effort into a losing battle to maintain discipline among bored, unruly youngsters.

What he couldn't understand was the attitude of his island friends. Every one of them seemed to look forward eagerly to going to school. Barney O'Neal, who had become a sort of hero to Rick, was among the most enthusiastic.

"Mr. Randall's goin' to give me some special work in science this year," he said. "What Oi want to be is a marine biologist—an' the colleges that have the best courses aren't easy to git into. So Oi've got to study up on my own."

"What's that—a marine biologist?" asked Rick. "An' why do you want to be one, instead of a Coast Guardsman or a tugboat skipper or something?"

"Marine biology," Barney explained, "is the study of fish an' everything that lives in the sea. Miss Hamilton's a marine biologist. But she doesn't know some o' the things Oi want to foind out. About shrimp, fer instance. Folks 'round here used to make a pretty good livin' shrimpin' in Pamlico Sound. Then somethin' happened. It got so, last year, they hardly caught any. An' they're still moighty scarce. What became of 'em? Did they jes' take it in their heads to go some place else? Or did some other koind o' fish mommick 'em?"

"Gee," said Rick, "if you could find out an' bring 'em back, you'd be helpin' everybody on Ocracoke!"

"Yeah," Barney said with a sigh. "But Oi've got a heck of a ways to go first."

On the opening day of school, Mrs. Landon got her sons ready with as much thoroughness as if they were going to church. "I didn't care so much in Brooklyn," she said. "But here everyone knows us. So you'll start, at least, with a clean shirt apiece."

They had also been to the little barbershop, where they were given close-cropped haircuts in honor of the start of school. Rick dragged his feet somewhat on the short walk, while Joey, who wasn't old enough to know better, ran eagerly ahead. Boys and girls were waiting in the yard, and Rick spotted Judy Ann among them.

She greeted him with a laugh. "You look different with a butch clip," she said. "But I like it, anyway. I'm sorry we won't be in the same room this year. Have to wait till next fall, when I'm in ninth grade."

Inside the building, Rick was due for a surprise. His home room, where the ninth and tenth sat, was big and light, with plenty of windows. Along one wall were shelves filled with books that looked inviting. The desks weren't new but well-kept and polished. And the whole school was on one floor, with an outside entrance to every room. Best

116

of all, the teacher who stood facing them was his friend, Mrs. Richards, young Andy's mother.

He found a seat next to Jed Rowan and sat down. After they had saluted the flag and sung one verse of "America," Mrs. Richards smiled at them.

"Something tells me," she said, "we're going to have a good year. I know you boys and girls well enough to be sure you'll all try hard, so now we can all get down to studying. Jed, please pass out these books."

The morning went well. Only once or twice did Rick find his attention straying, when a pony ambled past outside. While the tenth-graders were reciting, those in the ninth did their studying. At first, the city boy found this a distraction. His friends were used to it after years under the same system, and it didn't take long for him to learn to concentrate as they did.

There was a different feeling here about doing one's work well in school. Instead of being jeered at or called teacher's pets, the brighter students were actually admired. And this attitude was catching. Before long Rick was studying harder, so that he could do as well as Jed or Coley. He wasn't conscious of it at first, but after a week, when Mrs. Richards gave him a word of praise for a short theme he had written, he realized it made him feel good all over.

Even the first day brought some change in his thinking. When his mother asked him how he liked school, he cheerfully answered, "It's okay." And he meant it.

Chuck Styron had brought an old football to school. In the sandy open lot behind the building there was too little space for a regular football field, but the boys had room to pass and run, block and tackle. Rick was able to hold his own with the others, for the summer had given him some muscle and he was fairly fast.

Every afternoon, as long as the warm weather lasted, the boys played football after classes were out, then went to the

117

beach or the Sound for a swim. Homework didn't seem so hard after that much fun.

There was only one thing that marred Rick's enjoyment. Windy Jenkins seemed to hold some kind of grudge against him and missed no opportunity to show it. Perhaps it was because Rick had been taken in so wholeheartedly by the island boys, while Jenkins was still unpopular. Once or twice they came close to blows. Rick would bristle up at some slighting reference to "Yanks" or "Brooklyn Bums," and only the quick intervention of some of the other boys kept the two apart.

The films of the jamboree hadn't been ready in time for the first Scout meeting, but on the evening when the troop gathered for the second one, Chief O'Neal was on hand at the recreation hall with his projector. They settled down in the dark to watch.

The movie had turned out remarkably well. There were loud cheers when Andy Richards appeared on the screen and went through his trick-riding routine. Then came the pyramid. And finally they saw the preparations for the square dance. The camera had been turned toward the saddled ponies, waiting behind the crowd. Suddenly Rick leaned forward, holding his breath. He had caught a fleeting glimpse of a figure that moved away from the palomino colt and ducked into the yaupon thicket. Then the picture swung back to the arena and the crowd, just as he saw Jed and himself hurrying toward Dandelion.

Neither Jed nor Coley seemed to have noticed. But just at that moment, somebody got up quietly behind them.

"Hey, where ye goin', Windy? . . . Down in front!" angry voices muttered.

Rick hadn't been certain till then. "Jed," he whispered, "I'm goin' outside. When it's over, ask the chief to run that part again—just where we were ready to mount up. Keep your eye on the palomino!"

118

"Heck," Jed replied, "don't you want to watch the dance pictures?"

But there was no answer. Rick had already slipped out. He moved softly around the corner of the moonlit building, keeping in the shadows. His ear caught the faint crackle of a twig, then the sound of footsteps moving off up the road. Running across the sand, barefooted, he had come within a few yards before the other boy heard him.

Jenkins whirled around. "Who's that?" he asked hoarsely. "What do you want?"

"So it was you!" Rick panted. "You stuck that sandspur under the colt's saddle!"

Windy saw that Rick was alone. "Okay," he said more boldly. "Whatcha goin' to do about it?"

"This!" Rick answered, and swung a fist with all his pent-up fury behind it. The blow caught Jenkins on the cheek, and for a second he was stunned. Then he came charging in, his face twisted in an ugly snarl. Rick went down under the bull-like rush, and they thrashed around on the ground until he could squirm free. The blind anger had left him now. He felt cool and steady. Facing a bigger adversary, he knew he had to make his speed count.

The next time Jenkins rushed him, he ducked under the flailing fists and drove a hard right and a left into the boy's middle. Windy gasped and dropped his arms to cover his stomach. And again Rick hit him in the face. This time his aim was better, for his opponent staggered backward and sat down hard, a dark stream pouring from his nose.

"Had enough?" Rick asked. But before there was any answer, Jed Rowan and Barney O'Neal came running up. Jed must have guessed why Rick had left and followed him.

"What the—" Barney started to ask. Then he caught sight of the boy on the ground.

"This guy come sneakin' up an' slugged me," Jenkins blubbered through thick lips.

"An' a moighty good job, too," Jed replied hotly. "Don't tell us ye didn't have it comin'. Of all the dirty tricks—torturin' a horse!"

"You'd better git along home," Barney told the fallen warrior. "Take a piece of oice an' hold it to the back of yer neck. That'll help stop yer nose bleedin'. Come on, Rick. Let's go back to the hall."

"Wait a sec'," said Rick. He went over and held out his hand to Jenkins. "No more hard feelings?" he asked. "I'm sorry about your nose."

Windy hesitated, then took the proffered hand. "Okay," he mumbled. "It was s'posed to be just a joke. I didn't go to hurt the pony."

Rick helped him up and he went away, dusting off his jeans. The rest of them returned to the Scout meeting.

120

Chapter Thirteen

Now that autumn was moving in, the people of the island drew closer together as they prepared for another winter. Freight boats from the mainland brought coal, fuel oil, and bottled gas into the harbor. Food supplies were stacked on pantry shelves. Potatoes and turnips and pumpkins were stored in sheds, raised well above the ground, for this was the season when hurricanes and flood tides could be expected.

Around the stove in Jack's store, Rick heard some of the old-timers talk about storms and shipwrecks of other years. He began to understand why the Outer Banks had been called the "graveyard of the Atlantic." Several times, on rides up the beach with the troop, he had seen old remnants of wrecks—rusty, barnacle-crusted plates of steamers, stumps of schooner masts thrusting up out of the surf on the reefs.

Several of the older men in the store had served with the Coast Guard, and before that with the Lifesaving Service. They remembered famous wrecks of their youth. Rick was lucky enough to be present when a bent, white-bearded old fellow named Jedediah Midgett described the end of the *George W. Wells*.

"Biggest sailin' ship ever wrecked on the coast," he said. "A six-masted schooner out o' Boston, she was, headed south fer Floridy in the fall o' 1913. No radio in them days, o' course, an' she got no warnin' about the hurricane comin'. It hit us on the third o' September, an' caught the *Wells* half way 'twixt Hatt'ras an' Ocracoke Inlet. The wind whipped every sail off her an' she broached to, with the seas a-pourin' into her hold. Oi was out on beach patrol, an' when Oi first soighted her, she was driftin' in through them twenty-foot breakers.

"Quick as Oi could git word to the station, the boys run the cart out an' brung the Lyle gun an' apparatus up opposite the ship. She lay broadside on, with the waves poundin' clean over her, an' two hunnerd yards or so from shore. We could see the sailors an' passengers, lashed in the riggin', clingin' on fer dear loife.

"Well, suh, we got the stand set up fer the gun an' foired a loine out. Durn' if the wind wa'n't blowin' so hard it stopped the shot roight in the air, an' the loine fell short. Seven more toimes we troied it, usin' bigger charges o' powder, an' on the last 'un we foinally got a loine acrost her. Know what happened then? It broke whoilst they was haulin' it in! Her skipper was a man named York, an' he had enough sense to make fast a loine to an empty keg an' heave it overboard. Soon as it floated ashore we grabbed ahold an' was able to rig our breeches buoy."

"How many folks was drownded?" someone asked.

Midgett paused before answering and shot a stream of tobacco juice neatly into the box of sawdust provided for the purpose.

"How many?" he replied. "Not a durn' soul! It took all day but we got ever'body off—fifteen men, three women, an' two little young 'uns. The *Wells* was a total loss, though. Too fur gone to be refloated, an' her hull jest laid there till foinally somebody set foire to it. She was in ballast, so there weren't no cargo to salvage."

He leaned back comfortably in his chair and looked

122

around at his audience. "Reckon there ain't many folks left that remembers the *Ariosto*," he said. "Oi was only a boy then, but Oi got to see the wreck. That was 'roun' Christmas toime, in 'noinety-noine. This *Ariosto* was a steam freighter, headin' up fer Norfolk with a cargo they say was worth a million an' a half dollars—mostly wheat, cotton, an' cottonseed. There was thirty men in the crew.

"Them days, there was rules for sea cap'ns, put out by the Loifesavin' Service. One of 'em was that they should never troy to land in their own boats as long as there was a chance o' gittin' help from shore. The skipper o' this steamer didn't pay no heed. First off, he must ha' been way off course, fer the ship hit a shoal an' grounded in the breakers, 'bout three moiles south o' Hatt'ras Inlet. He sent up distress signals, an' the beach patrol, up at the old north-end station, answered with a red flare to tell him help was comin'.

"The sea was heavy that noight, but there was no danger the steamer would break up. Jes' the same, them idjits lowered two boats, an' all but the cap'n an' a few men started rowin'. In a few minutes both boats was capsized. It was still dark when the loifesavin' crew got there, an' the first thing they saw was a sailor staggerin' along the beach. He was the only man out o' the capsized boats that managed to swim ashore. Not the only one saved, though.

"The loifesavers set up their gun an' foired a shot. It fell way short, but when they hauled it back, there was somethin' heavy on the loine. Pretty soon they pulled out a man 'bout half drownded. Lucky fer him, the loine had dropped square acrost him an' he hung on. After that they drug one more feller out, an' when dayloight come, they managed to git a breeches buoy rigged to the ship. It wa'n't too hard to take off the skipper an' the other crewmen. But twenty-one pore seamen drownded, jes' because he didn't foller the rules. There was bodies washin' up on the beach fer days."

A younger man spoke up. Rick recognized him as one of the many O'Neals in Ocracoke. "Any o' you folks remember the wreck o' the schooner *Deering?*" he asked. "The one they called the ghost ship?"

There was a chorus of "sho' dos" and "yes, indeeds."

"Bow end used to be on our beach," Midgett answered with a nod. "They say she first went aground up Hatt'ras way, in a ca'm sea. Nobody aboard but the cat when the Coast Guard went out to her."

"That's roight," said O'Neal. "Decks swabbed, ropes all coiled down, ever'thin' shipshape. After the next storm, she broke in two, an' one part drifted down to lodge on Ocracoke. Washed away in one o' the hurricanes in 'fifty-foive, an' floated back up to Hatt'ras."

"Whatever happened to her crew?" Rick couldn't help asking.

Midgett shrugged. "Who knows, boy?" he replied. "Some thinks 'twas a pestilence killed 'em. Some says a mutiny."

"Uncle Oike," said O'Neal, "had a different oidea. He jes' figgered she run aground on the shoal, an' her skipper an' crew got fooled, seein' there was so little wind. Took to their boats an' started fer shore. But it don't take much of a sea to turn a boat over, an' moy Uncle Oike thought that's what must ha' happened."

The talk of wrecks went on while Rick listened, fascinated.

" 'Tain't the same nowadays," old Midgett concluded with a shake of his head. "Coast Guard's got all sorts o' newfangled gadgets—radio an' helicopters an' such. But, by gum, when a ship's aground in a hoigh sea, there's still nothin' kin take the place of a surfboat with a good crew at the oars. Ain't a powerboat built that kin put out from the beach through the koind o' breakers we git on the Banks."

*　　*　　*

The idea of trying to find pirate gold had stayed at the back of Rick's mind all summer. But as long as tourists were swarming over the island, he had put it off. At last, in late September, there came a Saturday when a chilly fog made riding and football unattractive. Instead of curling up indoors with a book, Rick stole out to the shed, got an old shovel, and made his way down toward Springer's Point. He knew he would be laughed at if any of the other boys saw him, so he took back lanes and paths through the woods.

He had begun reading again that fall, for there were many good books in the school library. Among other things, he had read everything he could find about Blackbeard, Stede Bonnet, and the other buccaneers who had once infested the coast. All the books seemed to agree that fleets of pirate vessels and their prizes had sometimes anchored in the relatively deep water of "Teach's Hole," where they were sheltered from northeast storms by the lower tip of the island. That they had come ashore, there was no doubt, and some authorities said Edward Teach had even put up a wooden watchtower from which he could spot ships approaching through Ocracoke Inlet.

Rick moved down the shore till he reached a little cove that seemed a natural place for the pirates to beach their boats. He had heard that inland a few hundred feet there was a small pool of fresh water. But he didn't think they would have gone there to drink their rum and divide their booty. It seemed more likely they'd build a driftwood fire on the beach, where they could loll in comfort, away from brambles and mosquitoes.

Rick looked around furtively, to make certain nobody was there to observe him, and thrust his shovel into the sand. For nearly an hour he worked steadily, till his arms ached and he was wet with sweat under his slicker. Once the spade struck metal, and he dug it up with breathless

eagerness. To his disgust it was nothing but a piece of rusty old automobile fender.

Glancing around him then, he realized that with all his labor he had turned over no more than a thousandth part of the desolate beach area, and only six or eight inches deep, at that. A few feet away, a small crab came out of its hole in the yellow-gray sand and looked at him with little pop eyes. He leaned on his shovel and laughed. Even if the pirates had been careless enough to drop a doubloon or two, they could stay there as far as Rick was concerned. He was cured of treasure-hunting for good.

On the way home he met Chuck Styron, who looked questioningly at the shovel. "Hm," he said. "Been doin' a little diggin', down 'long the point? What fer?"

126

"Clams," Rick replied with a straight face. "Didn't find a one, though."

The island boy chuckled. "Poor place fer 'em, at that. If ye want clams, Oi'll show ye where ye kin git a bushel. But not with a shovel. Mostly we use a clam rake."

Rick was pretty sure his friend knew what he had been digging for, and he was grateful that Chuck hadn't ribbed him about it.

"Thanks," he told him with a grin. "I'll take you up on that sometime."

When the mailboat came in that afternoon, Joey went to the post office and brought home a letter addressed to Rick. Mail was infrequent at their house. Miss Vronsky had written once or twice, and Rick had answered. But this

127

letter had a Florida postmark. With a thrill he looked at the sprawling handwriting. Back in July he had sent off a note addressed to Elmer Jukes, in Okeechobee, Florida. He had wanted to tell Slim about the palomino stallion.

"Dear Friend Rick," the letter began. "I was off on the circuit when yours of July 20 come to hand. I tole you that you had brung me luck and it keep on pretty good all summer. Right now I stand number 3 in calf roping and number 4 in saddel bronc riding. I judge you done real good yourself when you rid that Dandelion colt. May be I will see you in the rodeos some day. I never hered of that island you live on but with all them ponys it must be a plenty of fun liveing there. If you are still aiming to be a cowpoke may be I could get you a job on the ranch down here. Your friend Slim."

Rick didn't answer for a day or two. A few months earlier, he would have been wildly excited about Slim's idea. Now, to his surprise, he discovered it didn't appeal to him so much. He didn't know just why, but the thought of leaving Ocracoke troubled him. Not until he was in his seat in the classroom on Monday did the real reason come to him. Shocking as it might seem, he *liked* school!

When he finally answered Okeechobee Slim's letter, he thanked him for the offer but tried to explain why he must turn it down. "First of all," he wrote, "I'm not old enough. But even if I was bigger, I'd want to finish high school. The teachers here make you feel interested in learning things and I've got an awful lot to learn. I might even want to go to college if I'm smart enough to get a scholarship."

On an impulse he showed the letter to his mother before he mailed it. She read it thoughtfully, then smiled at him.

"Ricky," she said, "I'm going to stop worrying about you. Seems to me you've grown up quite a lot since we came here to live."

128

Chapter Fourteen

Through the summer Rick had been in and around boats a good deal. He was no longer seasick when he went out with Chuck or Coley, and he had learned to row and to handle a leg-o'-mutton sail. Nearly every family on the island owned a boat of some kind, even if it was only a flat-bottomed skiff.

Jed Rowan had such a boat, battered and long unpainted but reasonably watertight. He dropped by Rick's house one Saturday morning at the end of September.

"Got anything to do?" Jed asked. "Oi heard there's winter flounder on the shoals up beyond Horse Pen Point. Figgered we moight do some giggin'."

"Sure," said Rick. "I'd like to try it. Is it anything like fishing?"

"More fun, really," Jed told him with a grin. "All you need is a good eye an' quick hands. Come on—there's two gigs at home, an' you kin have one."

A gig, Rick discovered, was a sort of spear, with two or three steel prongs on the end of a long wooden shaft. The ones Jed produced were old and rusty, but a few minutes' work with a whetstone sharpened up the points. They carried the gigs down to the Rowan boat and were soon on their way out through the harbor entrance.

For several days the weather had been warm and sunny,

with hardly any wind. Some called it an early Indian summer. Others shook their heads and warned that it must surely be a weather-breeder. At any rate, the boys found Pamlico Sound almost as calm as a millpond that morning.

The water was clear, too. Sitting in the stern while Jed rowed, Rick could see the sand, five or six feet below, and the quick, darting movements of minnows and crabs. The skiff moved up the shore, past Mary Anne Pond and Northern Pond, swung up around a shallow bar and headed eastward. Soon the trees and brush dropped astern. They passed a couple of narrow sandspits and saw the flat, empty stretch of the plains that ran all the way up the island to First Hammock.

Jed pulled in the oars and peered over the side. "Ought to foind 'em along in here," he said. "Yeah, there's one ahead."

Quietly he picked up his gig and waited, while the boat drifted nearer. He poised the long handle above the water and drove it downward in a quick, hard thrust.

"Got him!" he said, and lifted a squirming two-pound flounder into the boat.

Every few yards, along the bottom, Rick could see the flat fish only three or four feet below. The way Jed had handled the gig made it look easy, and he gripped his own, waiting for a chance. The skiff moved slowly, making scarcely a ripple. When there was a flounder just beyond him, Rick lifted the spear and stabbed downward. He missed his target by several inches.

Jed laughed. "Guess Oi should ha' warned ye," he said. "Things under water ain't where they look to be. It's the refraction o' loight. Mr. Randall showed us in physics class. Ye have to allow fer it an' aim a little on the near soide."

Jed got two more fish before Rick mastered the art. After that he managed to keep up with the island boy, flounder

130

for flounder. When the school took alarm and moved to a
new basking place, they followed. By eleven o'clock they
had gigged more than a dozen fine big fish.

A puff of wind came over the island from the east and
ruffled the water so they could no longer see the bottom.
Several gulls flew past above them, screaming noisily. Jed
looked off to seaward and frowned.

"Skoy's gittin' sort o' dirty out there," he said. "Oi
reckon we'd best be headin' back."

There was only one pair of oars in the skiff, but they
took turns, one rowing, the other poling. Rick found it
more work each time he had the oars, for the wind blew
harder from moment to moment, and even in the lee of the
land there were choppy seas. By the time they were off the
harbor mouth, the whole eastern half of the sky had dark-
ened ominously.

Jed was rowing when they pulled toward the narrow
channel, right into the teeth of the wind and the outflowing
tide. He heaved mightily on the oars, but each stroke carried them only a little way forward. Waves began breaking
over the bow, and Rick went to work with the bailing
can. It took a good twenty minutes to get inside the sheltered basin.

"Golly gee!" Jed shouted, through the howl of the wind.
"This here's somethin' big—a real he-one! Look at that
flag!"

On the tall crosstree mast by the Coast Guard station,
Rick saw the flag standing out flat, like a sheet of iron, its
free edge already whipped to tatters.

They got their fish out, pulled the boat up extra high on
shore, and turned it bottom up. Then they hurried for
home, panting as the gale tore at their clothes. Rick took
his flounder into the kitchen to clean them. His mother
made no objection, though the rule was that such chores
should be done outside.

"I'm glad enough to see you safe home," she said. "Uncle Dan came by to tell us there was a storm expected. He got it on the radio, I guess. Said it might hit us by noon—a hurricane, coming up from the West Indies. The Weather Bureau calls it 'Helene,' though why they want to use girls' names, I'll never know."

Rick couldn't help giving her a smart answer. "I reckon it's because they're sort o' flighty," he said. "Contrary—always do the unexpected. But this one's sure right on schedule. You s'pose it'll do any damage?"

"No telling," his mother answered. "But I'll feel better when Joey's home. I'll finish the fish. You run over to Abel's house an' see if he's there."

At that moment Joey came in. "Gosh!" he said. "It's awful windy an' startin' to rain. Mis' Dennis sent me home. Said I might get blowed away if I didn't hurry."

They ate their midday meal to the accompaniment of

132

rattling windows and the roar of hard-driven rain on the shingles and siding. By the middle of the afternoon, Rick was restless. If this was to be a real hurricane, he wanted to see it. He put on his slicker and went outside.

The twisted cedars and live oaks had stood up to many winds before, and though they tossed their branches and groaned in anguish, they seemed to be surviving. Out of the lee of the house, Rick found he could barely keep his feet. If he turned into the wind, his breath was blown away. There was a spine-tingling roar coming from the ocean, but he knew he could never make it if he tried to go in that direction. He reached the main street along Silver Lake and was swept along westward, clutching at fences and tree trunks to keep himself upright.

With a sick feeling he thought of the ponies, up the island. Dandelion might be in trouble—blown clear into the Sound. And there was nothing he could do to help. Miserable, he clawed his way to the shelter of the ice plant and looked across toward the Coast Guard station. The little harbor, usually so placid, was lashed to seething turmoil now. Through the flying rain and spray he could see two shrimp boats that had torn loose from their moorings and piled up in the angle by the long wharf. They heaved and pounded against each other, but the roar of the storm drowned out their crashings.

As Rick crouched there, he suddenly saw the big door go up at the Coast Guard boathouse. It seemed impossible that anybody would launch a boat in such weather, but there it came—the big self-bailing surfboat, with a dozen men in oilskins rolling it down the ramp. In a moment it was in the water and the crew had scrambled aboard. The powerful engine went into action, and the boat, pitching like a bronco, went surging out into the fury of the Sound. There could be only one reason. Somewhere out there a boat must be in trouble.

Hardly knowing how he did it, Rick staggered on till he was past the machine shop and the Park Service office. In the lee of the westward end of the building, he caught his breath and measured the distance across to the Coast Guard station. An empty oil drum that stood on the dock came hurtling past him, bouncing end over end, and brought up with a clang against the parking-lot fence.

Rick started at a run. Twice he was flung down by the wind, but he picked himself up and went on, zigzagging crazily. At last he was behind the Coast Guard building. There was a back door that he and Jed had used on other visits, but he found it locked. One more short dash and he was in the boathouse.

"Hey!" cried a petty officer. "Where'd you come from?"

Rick knew the man—a bosun's mate called Shorty Enslow. He was alone in the boathouse, waiting for further orders after the launching of the surfboat.

134

"I—s-set out to see what it was like," Rick panted. "Blowin' so hard I couldn't get back." He leaned against the wall in a corner and felt the stout timbers shake to the buffeting of the blast. His slicker was still streaming water.

"What happened?" he asked. "I saw the boat go out."

"Got a radio signal," said Enslow. "Good-sized yacht aground on that shoal where the dredge sank a few years back. Won't take long to break her up in a sea like this."

"Gosh!" Rick said with a shiver. "I never knew a storm could be so bad. How hard's it blowing?"

"Last I heard, the wind was close to a hundred an' ten miles an hour, but I guess it's picked up some since then. It's sure blowin' as hard as I've ever seen it. Barometer's been droppin' fast, too. No question about this bein' a real hurricane."

Rick thought of the crew in the surfboat, out there in the tempest, and wondered if he would ever see them again. Some were probably friends of his.

"You reckon the boat can get back?" he asked. "Jed an' I had a bad time of it this morning—long before it really started to blow."

"It'll be rough," Shorty answered soberly. "But the tide turned a while back, an' it ought to be runnin' in by now. We're sure due fer a walloper of a high tide tonight. It might cover the whole island."

Again Rick had a mental picture of the ponies, knee-deep in rushing water, and his heart sank. Perhaps the tide would even be so high that it would flood the village. He ought to be home to help his mother in case of trouble, but one look outside told him he would have to wait.

There seemed to be no slacking in the terrible fury of the wind. It was after five o'clock now, and the boat had been gone nearly two hours. Already it was almost as dark as night. Shorty Enslow went to the light switch on the wall and turned it on. Nothing happened.

"Power's off!" he growled. "Couldn't ha' happened very long ago or they'd have started up our generator."

There came a flicker of light in the overhead lamp, and then it began to burn steadily. But when he looked out across the harbor, Rick saw that the village itself was dark.

"We have to have stand-by power here at the station," Enslow said. "Without the radio transmitter we'd be in a bad fix."

At that moment another Coast Guardsman came stumbling through the big open door. "Boat's been sighted," he gasped. "Her engine's dead, but they're rowin' her. Looks like they've got some survivors aboard."

The howl of the wind dropped suddenly to a moan, and they could make themselves heard without shouting.

"We're in the 'eye,'" said Enslow. "Won't blow fer a while, till the wind shifts. Come on—they'll be here 'fore long."

All three of them hurried out to the ramp. The air was strangely still and heavy. Through the narrow harbor entrance they could see the surfboat nosing into the waves, her crew pulling fiercely at the oars. A floodlight came on over the ramp, and in a few minutes the boat was brought alongside.

Four people—three men and a woman—crouched there, miserable and wet, among the rowers. As soon as they were helped ashore, one of the seamen was detailed to take them over to the main building. Meanwhile, tackle was made fast to the surfboat's stern, and she was hauled up the ramp into the boathouse.

"What sort o' vessel was it?" Enslow asked the Chief Petty Officer in charge of the rescue.

"Big cabin cruiser," he replied. "Forty-five footer named the *Daphne,* out o' New York. She'd broken up when we got there, an' they were hangin' onto a capsized dinghy. We hauled out the owner an' his wife an' two o' the crew.

136

There was one other—a Jap mess-boy. We couldn't find him, an' I reckon he was thrown overboard when she hit. Lucky the wind let up when it did or we'd still be out there breakin' our backs."

He pointed to Rick. "What's the kid doin' here?" he asked.

"Got blown all the way from the village," said Shorty with a grin. "Couldn't claw his way back, so he stayed here."

"Well," the Chief returned, "you'd better make tracks for home now, son, while you can. This calm may not last long."

Rick set off at a trot. He had begun to worry about his mother and Joey. As he went along the road, he could see the dim flicker of candles inside some of the houses. The great beam from the lighthouse that usually lit up the village was out. Only a faint sheen of moonlight, coming through the broken clouds, glimmered in the puddles on the road.

To his relief, the house was still there when he got home, and the glow of an oil lamp in the kitchen guided him across the wet yard to the back door. His mother sat at the plain deal table, an open Bible in front of her and Joey at her side. Her face was lined and haggard in the shadows.

"Gosh, Ma," said Rick hastily, "I'm sorry if you were worried. I couldn't get back against the wind, so I stayed at the Coast Guard station."

"It's all right, Ricky," she told him, trying to smile. "We didn't know what had happened to you, but as long as you're back, our prayers are answered. I haven't had the heart to start getting supper. 'Twon't take long, though."

While she busied herself at the stove, Rick described the wreck of the *Daphne* and the rescue by the surfboat crew.

"Gee!" Joey breathed. "Wish I'd seen it. That's what I'm goin' to be when I grow up—a surfman, just like Pa was."

They ate supper, and the boys did the dishes. It was while Rick was putting the last plate away that he heard the gurgle of water. It seemed to come from underneath the floor. With a shock he remembered that high tide was due at seven o'clock, and it was nearly that now. Quickly, he ran to a window and looked out.

Everywhere the moon shone on rushing, swirling water. It was over the road, over the yard, halfway up the picket fence. He opened the front door and saw sticks and debris floating by at the level of the second step. Another foot and it would reach the threshold!

Mrs. Landon had gone upstairs to see that Joey got to bed. Rick didn't want to alarm her, but it was his turn now to do some praying. This house was all they had. He asked God to keep it firm on its piling and not let the water come much higher. Then he added an afterthought. "Dear Lord," he murmured, "please take care o' the ponies an' lead 'em to high ground if there's any left."

As he finished, the west windows began to rattle. The calm at the center of the storm had gone past, and now the tail of the hurricane was lashing in from the landward side. As the wind gained strength, it whipped up foamy waves on the still-rising flood. Water splashed against the siding and came through in snaky puddles under the doors.

Rick rushed to get a mop. He was still swabbing away industriously when his mother came downstairs. The moment she saw what was happening, she began picking up all movable things from the floor and stacking them on the table.

"This is as bad as one we had when I was a girl," she said. "We'll just have to hope some o' the tide'll be washed back toward the beach, now that the wind's shifted."

For the better part of an hour Rick kept on mopping, barely able to keep ahead of the inflowing water. Then at last he found the trickle was growing less. It was pitch dark outside, but when he opened the rear door a crack, he could see that the flood had subsided a little.

His mother sank into a chair and smiled wanly. "I guess we can go to bed now," she said. "Time enough in the morning to clean up the mud an' mess."

Chapter Fifteen

Rick slept well from midnight on, in spite of the scream of the wind. When he woke, the storm was over and the sun was shining in at the window. The church bell rang with a glad note of thanksgiving.

"You boys dress up for Sunday School," Mrs. Landon called up the stairs. "I'm sure they'll have it, even if a lot of folks'll be out looking over the damage."

Rick grumbled only a little. He never liked wearing his best clothes, but at least he would have a chance to exchange experiences with some of his friends.

The water had drained away by nine o'clock, leaving only mud and flotsam in the roads and dooryards. Right in front of the house Rick found the bedraggled body of a drowned chicken. It was typical of many minor tragedies that had befallen the town. There was destruction everywhere. Gardens were washed out, trees and fences uprooted, shrubbery stripped of leaves and festooned with muddy seaweed. The Landon house had suffered less than most, losing only a few shingles and half a dozen bricks from the chimney.

Over at the church the boys found a smaller group than usual. Coley Fulcher was there, and Jed Rowan. Barney O'Neal, they told Rick, had been out all night helping people who were in trouble.

"They took close to fifty folks over to the Coast Guard station when the toide was full in," said Jed. "Water was so hoigh, the trucks an' jeeps could hardly git through. You oughta see the road down around the harbor. Bet there's a dozen gas boats an' skiffs hoigh an' droy, some of 'em roight in the street. An' more still got sunk, Oi reckon."

"Hear about the wreck out in the Sound?" Coley asked. "One man drowned an' the surfboat had a heap o' trouble savin' the rest."

"Yeah, I was there an' saw 'em when they came in," Rick was proud to reply. "What about the ponies? Anybody been up-island to see?"

The other two shook their heads. "That's got me worried, too," said Coley. "There were two or three of 'em 'round our house this mornin', lookin' moighty wet an' mournful, but Oi don't know how the main bunch made out."

"Well," Rick urged, "soon as Sunday School's over, let's go an' see."

An hour later they were on their way up the island. Jed had borrowed his father's jeep, and they rolled northeastward without trouble till they were a mile or so above the village. Then the highway disappeared almost completely. Much of it was buried deep in sand. Elsewhere the flood waters had undermined the roadway, and sections of it had sunk a foot or more.

They plowed along at five or six miles an hour, the engine laboring, through soft, wet sand. Ahead of them the storm-battered trees of First Hammock loomed up.

"Moight be some ponies there," said Coley. "Hammock Oaks is about as hoigh as any dune around."

They swung the jeep to the left and reached the slope of the wooded sand hill. Rick and Coley went up on foot. In among the trees were seven ponies, gnawing hungrily at leaves and twigs. To Rick's disappointment, Dandelion wasn't among them. The little horses seemed glad to see them and came forward, whinnying gently. The boys picked out two that wore the "K" brand and mounted them, knowing they could move at least as fast as in the jeep.

A few miles farther on, they came to a strange sight. Off to the eastward, roosting in the tops of a grove of cedars, were two huge steel barges. Rick and Coley rode over to them and read the battered lettering on the stern of the nearest one. "NEW BERN," it said.

"That's a long ways!" Coley exclaimed. "Must ha' broke loose from a dock or a tow an' been blown clean across the Sound. An' look at the soize of 'em! Way over a hundred foot long!"

They rode on, past Quork Hammock and Green Island and the Tar Hole Plains. "Yon's where they got to be—up in Styron's Hills," said Coley. "Anyhow, here's hopin'."

He was right. In the woods that covered the high dunes they found the main herd. Rick's heart was heavy at the sight of those woebegone ponies, but he felt much better when he caught a glimpse of the palomino. He gave the special whistle he had taught Dandelion to obey, and a moment later the colt was beside him, nosing at his hand.

"Poor little cuss!" he crooned. "I know I should ha' brought an apple, but I forgot."

He swung off the pony he had been riding and climbed aboard the palomino. "You and I," he said, "are going home where I can take care of you."

Coley, meanwhile, had been making a count. "Best Oi kin do is thirty-one," he said. "With those we saw further down, an' the ones around the village, that leaves six or seven short. One Oi don't see is that pretty little filly o' Gaskill's. Here, you count an' see what you git."

Rick moved through the herd carefully. The brown stallion had no fear now. He seemed as glad of human company as any of the others. When the boy finished his tally, it was the same as Coley's. Six, and possibly seven, of the little horses were missing. They rode back to Jed, where he sat in the jeep, near what had once been the highway. His face was long as he greeted them.

"Guess you found the ponies," he said. "But there's a couple we won't be roidin' again. Oi come on their bodies, a ways back." He jerked a thumb over his shoulder, and when they looked in that direction, they saw two forlorn dots lying in the sand. Rick shivered.

"There's more'n that missing," said Coley. "Some o' the ponies that belong to the troop are gone."

They were quiet on the ride down the island. It hurt to think of half a dozen friendly ponies lost in the storm. Rick wondered how the rest would make out, now that so much of their fodder had been flooded over by mud and sand, and their water holes pulluted with salt. Part of the question was answered when they stopped to rest near the Hammock Oaks. Dandelion sniffed the sand, pawed at it with his front hoofs, and scooped it out to a depth of a foot or more. The water that filled the depression couldn't have been too brackish, for he put his head down and drank eagerly. Sand must make a good filter.

Rick rode the young horse into the yard at home, gave him a couple of apples, and curried his muddy, matted hide. For the rest of the day, Dandelion was content to stay close to the house.

The school building had escaped flooding by inches, and classes opened as usual on Monday morning. Meanwhile, the whole village joined forces to help repair homes that had been damaged. A few hardy tourists went out fishing, though the swells were still running high. Other visitors from the mainland waited to get home as best they could, by freight boat or on the emergency ferry that soon began running once a day between Ocracoke Village and Hatteras.

When Rick came home from school, he found two neighbors up on the roof, patching shingles and rebuilding the chimney. They wanted no money for this work, and he felt the least he could do in return was offer to help them with their own repairs. So, for the rest of that week, he worked wherever he could. It was a community project, shared by everyone on the island. Within a matter of days the big clean-up task was finished, the stranded boats were back in the water, and most of the sunken craft were raised. Rick was proud to have been a part of it.

Through October, life went on as usual. There were no more hurricanes. Square dances and Scout meetings were held on weekends, and Rick took Judy Ann Fulcher to the movies once or twice.

It was early in November that he saw his first flight of ducks. Long before that, most of the other birds had left for Florida and South America. All the small waders were gone, together with the terns and the skimmers. For weeks he had seen no wild fowl except the noisy gulls. But one evening he heard a strange sound in the sky and looked up to see thousands of ducks winging over. Beyond the lighthouse, the huge flock broke up and settled in the marshes at the lower tip of the island.

A few weeks later the hunters began to arrive. Ocracoke was famous for its shooting—one of the favorite stops for ducks, geese, and brant along the coastal flyway. On the day before the season opened, the Wahab Village Hotel was filled to overflowing with gunners who had come in by ferry or small plane, ready to start at the crack of dawn. Some of the men and older boys in the village would be working as guides.

It was rainy, cold, and blowy in the morning, with a wind from the southeast. Ideal duck-hunting weather, Rick heard people say. Beginning with the first daylight, there was a steady banging of guns in the distance.

144

That evening, he was doing his homework by the kitchen lamp when Jed Rowan came to the back door. Jed had been hurrying.

"There's a hunter missin'," he panted. "Didn't come back with the others at suppertoime. They've asked the Scouts to help with the search. Kin you come?"

"Sure," said Rick promptly. "Got any ponies to ride?"

"There's half a dozen of ours, 'round town here. Oi saw Dandelion down the road a piece an' brung him along."

Within a minute Rick was ready. He told his mother where he was going, pulled on his jacket, and jumped on the palomino's back. They rode to Captain Howard's house, where four or five other Scouts had gathered.

"This man's name is Trimble," the captain told them. "He was with three other hunters when they set out. The rest of 'em got in the blinds around Old Hammock Creek, but he went off by himself. Said he wanted to try further up. That was about seven o'clock in the morning, an' they haven't seen him since. I reckon we'd better start at First Hammock an' work up along the marsh."

Jed, Coley, and Rick rode together. As soon as they passed Sand Hole Creek, they began to see other searchers, usually men on foot, carrying lanterns. It had stopped raining, and now the moon came out through the breaking clouds. There was enough light to show them where they were going.

Beyond Quork's Point the boys separated, each covering a fifty-yard strip of marsh. They passed empty duckblinds, and a shack or two, as they worked along the banks of the tidal creeks. Every few minutes, they heard the quacking of ducks where the flocks rested on the water.

It was a long, slow job, for the creeks twisted and turned all through the marsh. Rick was slowly skirting one of the arms of Try Yard Creek when the colt shied suddenly and gave a snort. The reeds were high along the bank, but Rick thought he saw something dark at the edge of the water.

"So-o, boy—stand easy," he admonished the palomino, and swung down to investigate. As he parted the marsh grass, he heard a sound like a faint groan. Then he saw the man. He was lying in an awkward position, one leg half submerged in the rising tide. When Rick bent over him, he could barely hear him breathing.

"Jed—Coley!" the boy yelled. "He's here! I've found him!"

While he waited for them to come, he looked around in the marsh grass. Lying a few feet away was a beautiful shotgun, its silver mountings shining in the moonlight. The man moaned again and tried to move.

"Lie still," Rick told him soothingly. "There's help on the way. We've got to find how bad you're hurt before we can move you."

He had remembered that much from his Scout First Aid training. In another moment the other two boys cantered up and dismounted.

"There's a patch o' what looks like blood under his right leg," Rick told them in a low voice. "I reckon he must have shot himself by accident. Probably he's bled a lot. What had we better do?"

"Haul him out o' the water first," Coley answered. "Then roide fast an' git a jeep out here."

Very gently they put their hands under the hunter's arms and pulled him back a yard or two.

"I'll go," said Rick. "You stay here with him."

He rode Dandelion out of the marsh onto hard sand and went down the island at full gallop. Whenever he encountered other searchers, he shouted the news. Near the Hammock Oaks he saw an empty jeep standing near the roadway. Several blasts on the horn brought two men from the marsh on the run, and a moment later he was leading the way back to the wounded gunner.

Jed and Coley had applied a tourniquet to the man's leg by the time the jeep arrived, but he was still unconscious and weak from loss of blood. All five of them carried him carefully to the little car. They laid him crosswise in the back seat, with his leg on a pile of hunting coats to soften the jolting. Then the boys rode toward the village as fast as their ponies could carry them.

Jed headed for the hotel to tell Mr. Trimble's friends he had been found. Coley went to get Miss Craig, the village nurse, and Rick took the word to the Coast Guard station. At once, Chief O'Neal called the mainland to send a helicopter and a surgeon. They arrived within an hour, and soon after midnight Rick had seen the injured man carried aboard the 'copter and started on his way to a hospital in Elizabeth City. As he had guessed, Trimble had tripped and shot himself, smashing both bones of his lower leg. He had

147

lost so much blood that the doctor said he would have died in another two hours if he hadn't been found.

Rick sat in civics class next morning, a little sleepy after his night's activities. Mrs. Richards looked his way.

"Ricky Landon," she said, "what can you tell us about the first ten amendments to the Constitution?"

That was what he was supposed to have studied for homework. He got up, cleared his throat, looked at his feet, and wondered hazily what those amendments were called. But before he had time to answer, there came a knock at the door. Mr. Randall entered, followed by three strangers.

"Sorry to interrupt you, Mrs. Richards," the principal said with a smile. "These gentlemen would like to speak to Rick Landon. Ah—I see he's already on his feet."

All three men stepped forward and shook hands with the confused boy. "I'm John Townsend," one of them said. "Jeff Trimble is my business partner, and these are two more of his friends. We understand it was you who found him last night and probably saved his life. We've made up a little purse amongst us, and we'll be happy if you'll accept it."

Rick's mouth fell open, and he could feel the color rising in his cheeks. He tried to shake his head, but his classmates were on their feet, cheering.

"That's all right, Rick," said Mr. Randall kindly. "You don't have to make a speech. Just take the money. Seems to me you deserve it."

Hesitantly, Rick took the envelope Mr. Townsend put in his hand and said "Thank you." Then the men were gone. He was still standing there in a daze when the answer to Mrs. Richards' question suddenly popped into his head.

"The Bill o' Rights!" he blurted out. And everybody in the classroom roared.

148

Chapter Sixteen

There were five ten-dollar bills in the envelope when Rick finally opened it. That was more money than he had ever held in his hand—far more than he had ever owned. At first he tried to give some to Jed and Coley, but they insisted it was he who had found the wounded hunter and it belonged to him.

On his mother's advice, he used the fifty dollars to start a Postal Savings account.

"It would be easy enough to spend it, goodness knows," she said. "But now that I'm earning a little, we won't suffer. Put it where it'll draw interest, an' it'll be there when you really need it."

The weeks before Christmas were full of plans and preparations. Both the churches would be having Christmas programs, but most of the youngsters' activities were centered in the school. Joey's room was going to present a pageant of Bethlehem, with a stable scene and a real, live cow. Joey would be one of the shepherds. He made his own crook out of a twisted cedar limb, and his mother fashioned his robe and headdress from an old sheet.

Rick, meanwhile, was helping to build sets and paint scenery for the high school's show. This was to be a complete TV program—live, of course—as telecast from "Station OCRA." There would be announcers, commercials, interviews, songs, jokes, and dances, climaxed by the arrival of Santa Claus in person. One of the highlights was a fashion show, with Sally Dennis and Judy Ann Fulcher modeling the "latest Paris creations." Another was an impersonation of a famous wriggle-hipped crooner, done by Johnny Garrish with his guitar.

Rick, himself, sang in a barbershop quartet. He could contribute a passable tenor and a good ear, both somewhat rare in a group whose voices were changing.

All through the final week they worked like dogs, sometimes until late at night, but they loved every minute of it. Rick still had a little money left from summer earnings, and he spent it now for Christmas presents. At the Community Store he got a toy truck for Joey and a sturdy aluminum frying pan he knew his mother needed. His last dollar went for a small locket, which he gave Judy Ann on the final day of school, when gifts were being exchanged. Her present to him was a box of cookies she had baked herself.

The show was held in the recreation hall before a packed audience. Nervous at first, the youngsters responded to the laughter and applause and outdid themselves. Everybody voted it the best entertainment the village had seen in a long time.

With the beginning of the holidays, Rick was able to do what he liked with his time. Twice he went fishing with Jed Rowan and Chuck Styron, pulling in enough bottom fish to sell as well as to eat. Then, three days before Christmas, Barney O'Neal came by and invited him to go duck-shooting. Barney had his own gun and had borrowed a light twenty-gauge from his father. His dog, Rusty, an old Chesapeake Bay retriever, accompanied him.

"Better dress good an' warm," he told Rick. "It gits pretty chilly out there when you have to set still a spell."

150

They hiked three or four miles up the island and went out on the marsh to a spot Barney knew. There was no blind, but the reeds were tall enough to screen them when they were crouched down. The weather was cloudy, with spits of rain coming in on an easterly wind.

Rick had never handled any kind of gun, and he paid close attention while Barney showed him how to load, carry, and aim it, and how to "lead" a bird that was flying across his sights.

"Too bad you couldn't have had a couple o' practice shots," said the older boy. "But Oi wouldn't want to do any bangin' that moight scare off a floight."

Just in front of them was a little sheltered cove, where ducks might be expected to settle. Two or three times they saw small flocks beating down the edge of the island, but they flew on, too high for a shot. At last Barney pointed northward to a larger flock flying in over the Sound and quacking as they came.

"They're talkin' it over," he whispered. "Git ready."

Rick raised the twenty-gauge gun with trembling hands. He saw the ducks come closer, veering into the wind and dropping for a landing on the water close by. Barney's gun roared, first one barrel, then the other. Two ducks fell. The rest went up with a frightened whirring of wings before Rick could aim.

"Next toime they'll be yours," said Barney. "Go fetch, Rusty!"

The retriever broke out of the reeds and took a long, leaping plunge into the icy water. In a minute he had brought back both the ducks. Then he went off a few yards, shook himself thoroughly, and lay down once more.

"Canvasbacks," said Barney. " 'Bout the best eatin' there is."

The day was drawing toward dusk, and the weather

151

grew steadily worse. Rick shivered under his sweater and jacket, wishing he had put on a slicker as well. Suddenly Barney stirred.

"Listen!" he whispered, and Rick heard a faint, far-off honking. Rusty heard it too and whined eagerly.

"Honkers," said Barney. "Canada geese. There they are —see the 'V'?"

The geese were very high and still a long way off, but Rick could make out their formation dimly through the rain.

"If they come in here," Barney whispered, "that gun'll be too small. Here—take moine."

Although Rick protested, Barney thrust the twelve-gauge into his hands, and they waited tensely. With a quickening heartbeat, Rick realized that the geese were dropping, coming nearer. A great, handsome gander led them down, braked with his wings, and swung eastward not thirty yards away.

152

"Let him have it!" said Barney, and Rick pulled the front trigger. The recoil knocked him off balance, but Barney grabbed the gun out of his hands and fired the second barrel.

"Yippee!" he cried. "Two of 'em! We each got one!"

Rick rubbed his shoulder. "Boy!" he laughed. "I sure don't know how I hit him. That gun's got a kick like a mule!"

The Chesapeake brought the two big birds ashore, and the boys started home with their bag. The gander, so proud and beautiful a few moments before, hung heavy in Rick's hand. He thought then that he wouldn't much care if he never killed another one.

Barney seemed to understand how he felt. "Too bad, in a way," he remarked. "But don't fergit—you're takin' home a real foine Christmas dinner!"

*   *   *

The two weeks of vacation slipped away, and early January found Rick back in school. He worked hard to keep up his good record in class, but there was time for fun, too. Each of the four high school grades had its own basketball five, and they played one another almost every afternoon.

The recreation hall wasn't quite big enough for a full-sized court. They solved that by installing a single basket and backboard. Whichever team had possession of the ball could shoot, so all the action naturally centered at that end of the floor. The Seniors and Juniors had the most height. They used it to advantage in getting rebounds away from the lower class teams, but they couldn't shoot any better. And, when it came to fast dribbling and passing, some of the smaller boys could more than hold their own. They had some exciting games and plenty of good exercise.

The weather never got very cold on the island. It was too

close to the edge of the Gulf Stream, and snow was a rarity. Late in February, they did get one freak snowstorm. It came out of the southwest and blanketed the village with nearly six inches of soft white flakes. But by noon the next day all but a few remnants were gone.

Rick and Joey, of course, were experts at making and throwing snowballs. They had a grand time at first, pelting their schoolmates. Then some of the others learned the art and concentrated their attack on the Northerners. The only casualty was one window in the seventh- and eighth-grade room. Everybody thought it was Windy Jenkins who was responsible, but since he refused to admit it, they passed the hat to pay for a new pane of glass.

By early March there were real signs of spring. Buds began to open on many of the trees, northward-bound robins chirped in the dooryards, and snowdrops and crocuses were in bloom. For several days, the sun was so warm that some of the boys started going barefoot. Rick even tried the water in the Sound and was tempted to go swimming. Before he could get his trunks, however, the wind shifted and a cold rain began to fall.

It drizzled for two days, then cleared and grew warm again. Rick encountered Chuck Styron after school and suggested a fishing trip on the coming Saturday. Chuck counted on his fingers, then shook his head.

"Sorry," he said. "Oi couldn't take the boat out this Sat'day."

There was something sheepish about the way he spoke, and Rick didn't ask why. He supposed Chuck must have done something his father didn't like and was being punished for it. Not until Saturday itself, when he saw that not a single boat had gone out, did he remember the date. It was "Old Quork's Day!"

Half a dozen men were loafing on the pier beside Jack's store, and Rick heard the sound of a portable radio. "Here's

154

the latest weather report," an announcer was saying. "A storm of considerable force is now centered off Charleston and moving up the coast. Gale winds from the northeast may be expected. Storm warnings are up from Cape Fear to Hampton Roads."

One of the men on the dock, the owner of a shrimp boat, got up and stretched. "Guess Oi'll go put double moorin's on the *Sally Jane,*" he said. And, one by one, the fishermen followed his example. The last one was Hank Styron, Chuck's father. He gave Rick a grin.

"No use to buck the weather, come Ol' Quork's Day," he said. "She'll be blowin' plenty in another hour or so."

The sky had been hazy when Rick got up that morning. Now it was a dirty gray to the south and east, and even before he reached home, the wind had come. By nightfall it was up to sixty miles an hour, and the rain was driving past in level sheets.

Mrs. Landon wasn't worried. "It's no hurricane," she said. "Wrong time o' year. Just a good, stiff northeast storm. Could be it'll last a couple more days."

In that, at least, she was wrong. By ten o'clock on Sunday the wind and rain had stopped and the skies were clearing rapidly. Jed Rowan was waiting for Rick when he came out of the church.

"Oi aim to go fer a roide up the beach," he said. "Want to go along?"

"You bet," Rick agreed. "Just as soon's I can change my clothes."

Dandelion had been in the yard all night. After the fall hurricane, he had seemed to feel that the Landon place was where he belonged in rough weather. Rick put a bridle on him, met Jed at the gate, and they rode across to the ocean side of the island. The seas breaking on the beach were still mountain-high, but the tide was out. By some freak of the storm, a huge gully had been washed out along the tide

155

line, leaving cliffs of sand on the land side so steep the ponies had to slide down practically on their tails.

"Maybe we'll find a wreck if we go up far enough," said Rick. "Some ship driven ashore by the wind."

Jed was scornful. "Guess the Coast Guard would ha' heard about it," he replied. "Don't git so many wrecks nowadays. Freighters an' tankers gen'ally give the Banks a woide berth."

"But," Rick argued, "some old wreck might ha' worked loose from where she lay. Look how the beach has been washed out."

They rode five or six miles without seeing any promising wreckage. Then Jed wanted to turn back. "Maw's havin' dinner at two o'clock," he said. "She'll skin me if Oi ain't home."

"Go ahead," Rick told him. "We don't eat till four on Sunday, so I'm going on a way."

Since nothing big enough to be the hull of a ship was in sight ahead, Rick dismounted and led the pony up the beach. He was interested in the strange shells and other buried objects that had been scoured out by the storm. In the back of his mind was the thought that a pirate chest might be among them, but nothing so romantic appeared.

Once he did find a huge old oak timber, worm-eaten and crusted with barnacles, and there was also a foot-long link of anchor chain, badly rusted. He had gone two-thirds the length of the island when he decided it was time to turn back. He went around to the colt's left side and was preparing to mount when something in the bottom of the gully by his foot caught his attention. It looked like the brass-tipped spoke of a ship's steering wheel.

He reached down to pick it up, but found it was firmly imbedded in the sand. Digging with his hands, he came to the curved rim of the wheel and two more spokes attached to it. At last he was able to loosen the whole frag-

156

ment and lift it out. The broken arc appeared to be about a third of the whole wheel. It was made of some dark, heavy wood that he thought might be teak, and though the brass fittings were green with verdigris, the wood itself seemed to be remarkably sound.

The relic would be an awkward thing to carry, and he was about to throw it away. Then he thought better of it. Perhaps Captain Howard or Mr. Randall might be interested. Tucking it under his arm, he rode the palomino up the steep bank and cantered off down the sands. When he reached home, he dropped the piece of wheel in a corner of the kitchen and washed up for dinner.

It was Joey who reminded him of it later that evening. The younger boy was scraping industriously at something on the rim of the wheel.

"Look, Rick," he piped, "there's letters on it. I think it says 'U.S.S. MO'—then a few more letters an' an 'R.' "

"Let's see," said Rick. He noticed for the first time that there was an eroded brass plate on the flat side of the rim. Joey had dug away some of the greenish crust and exposed the engraved lettering. Quickly Rick took it to the sink and used scouring powder and a scrub brush to lay bare more of the plate. Then he rinsed it off. Under his astonished eyes the worn letters came out—"U.S.S. MONITOR."

The *Monitor,* he thought, trying to remember his history. Wasn't she the little "cheesebox on a raft" that had fought a battle with the *Merrimac* in the Civil War? Perhaps this had come from some less famous ship with the same name. Anyhow, he would show it to Mr. Randall in the morning.

Chapter Seventeen

Rick wrapped the wheel fragment carefully in an old newspaper and carried it to school with him. Going in before the bell rang, he found the principal busy at his desk. When he looked up, Rick asked if he could bother him a minute.

Mr. Randall grinned. "Certainly, Rick, any time. What have you got there? Not a dead fish, I hope."

"No, sir. But I did find it on the beach, an' I wanted to know what you think of it." He unwrapped his treasure and laid it on the desk. For a moment the older man stared at the inscription, then brought his fist down with a bang.

"By George!" he exclaimed. "It looks real enough! Where was it when you found it?"

Rick explained about the deep gullies in the beach. "I figure it might ha' been buried there for years," he said, "until this last storm. What bothers me is how it ever came to be on Ocracoke."

Mr. Randall sprang up and went with long strides to the bookcase. He returned with a copy of *Graveyard of the Atlantic* by David Stick.

"We'll find the story here," he said, turning the pages rapidly. "You see, after her big fight with the *Merrimac* and some campaigning in the James River, the Federal Navy decided to send the little *Monitor* down to Charleston, where she could be of more use. Right after Christmas, in 1862, she set out from Fort Monroe in company with the steamer *Rhode Island*. The weather was bad when they started, and it got worse. By the time they were off Cape Hatteras it was blowing a full gale. The *Monitor* was never too seaworthy, and with the seas rolling clear over the turret, she took in so much water the engine room was flooded. There was no power to pump her out. Meanwhile, the *Rhode Island* had taken her in tow. But the only way they had of signaling between the ships was a blackboard they held up. When it grew dark, the night of the thirtieth, of course the blackboard was no use. The *Monitor* kept on filling with water till she had to be abandoned. She carried no boats, but her crew showed a red light that was finally seen aboard the steamer.

"Two lifeboats were launched from the *Rhode Island* and rowed through those wicked seas to the ironclad's turret, which was still above water. All the men still alive were in it and on top of it. The boat crews took most of them off—all they could carry—and made it back to the steamer, where they had a rough time getting them aboard. Then one of the lifeboats went off into the storm to try to pick up the rest of the *Monitor*'s men. That was the last the *Rhode Island* saw of her. The empty boat was picked up later at sea, but her crew must have drowned, along with twelve men and four officers who went down with the ironclad.

"Now, Rick, the place where all this happened was ten miles east of Cape Hatteras—only about twenty miles from our upper beach. Another thing is that the helmsman of the *Monitor* that night—a sailor named Francis Butts, who was saved—said they had taken the wheel from its regular place in the little pilothouse on the forward deck, and rigged it temporarily on top of the turret. That means it could easily have broken away when the vessel sank.

"I'm convinced you've made an important find, Rick, and if you don't object, I'll write to the Mariners' Museum, in Virginia. I think we ought to get their opinion."

Rick had stood there drinking in every word, his eyes getting bigger and bigger. "Sure, Mr. Randall," he said at last. "I guess they'd know. Maybe you'd better keep it here, in a safe place, until you hear from 'em. Young Joey was playing with it last night."

The principal laughed. "Quite a boy, that brother of yours. I'll put your find right here, in this big drawer, and lock it up. And I'll let you know as soon as I get an answer."

Rick said nothing to the other Scouts about his discovery, and he threatened Joey with dire consequences if the younger boy breathed a word. He dreaded being laughed at if the broken wheel turned out to be a fake or a relic of some less renowned ship.

The week went by, and no word came from the museum. Mr. Randall told Rick not to worry—that the people up there probably had a lot of other things to do and would get around to answering in due time. But it was a letdown after his first glow of excitement.

On Saturday morning Rick was down at the store when the ferry from Hatteras came chugging into the harbor. A temporary slip had been built, near the marine engine shop, and Rick went over there to see her come in. As usual, the boat was heavily loaded with cars, in addition to Rufe Steele's truck. Watching idly from the roadside, Rick saw twelve local cars rattle down the steep-pitched ramp. The thirteenth bore Virginia license plates. The driver hesitated, then pulled over near where Rick stood. He was a gray-haired, mousy little man in spectacles.

"I beg your pardon," he said. "I'm a stranger here. Could you direct me to a Mr. Edward Randall's residence?"

160

Rick gulped. "Yes, sir," he said. "It isn't too easy to find. Maybe I'd better come with you."

After he was in the car, he got up enough assurance to put his question. "Are—are you from the Mariners' Museum?" he asked.

"Why, yes," said the man, surprised. "I'm sure I don't know how you guessed it, though."

"I'm the boy who found the *Monitor*'s wheel," Rick replied. "I took it to Mr. Randall, an' I knew he wrote to you. We've been hoping somebody would answer."

"Hm," said the man, "perhaps I should have written, but it seemed too important to handle by mail. So you found it, eh? Want to tell me about it?"

Rick did his best to describe the gullies washed out of the beach by the storm. "I guess there were shells an' stuff there that hadn't been uncovered in a good many years," he said. "I was a long way up—maybe four or five miles below Hatteras Inlet—when I saw one o' the wheel spokes sticking up out o' the bottom o' the gully. It wasn't till I got it home that I noticed the brass plate, but when I scrubbed it, the letters came up clear enough—'U.S.S. MONITOR.' I think Mr. Randall's kept it at the schoolhouse, but we'd better pick him up first."

A moment later they reached the principal's house and knocked at the door. Mr. Randall came in his shirtsleeves, his eyes twinkling behind his glasses.

"My name's Clausen," said the man with Rick. "I'm an associate curator at the museum—here in answer to your letter."

"Good!" Mr. Randall replied. "Be with you in a jiffy."

They drove back around the harbor to the school and were soon examining the old piece of steering wheel. Mr. Clausen took a magnifying glass from his pocket and studied the wood and the brass intently. For a while he

made no comment, and Rick, watching him, had an un-
happy feeling that there was something wrong.

"The wood appears to be teak, all right," said Mr. Clausen at last. "And the plate gives every evidence of having
been buried a long time in salt sand. I'd like to check the
location, though. Do you have a large-scale map of the
Outer Banks?"

"Better than that," Mr. Randall told him. "I've got the
Geodetic Survey charts."

He unrolled five or six of the big sheets, showing all of
Ocracoke and the lower end of Hatteras Island.

"It was right about here I found it," said Rick, putting
his finger on a spot nearly opposite Patch Fence Creek.
"I remember I'd gone just a little way past Quork Hammock."

Clausen nodded. He asked for a ruler and laid it on the
map. "The best records we have," he said, "show that the
Monitor went down in fifty or sixty fathoms, just north of
Diamond Shoals. That would be only about twenty miles
east-northeast of the place you say you found the wheel on
Ocracoke. Certainly it's a logical direction for bits of wreck-
age to drift. We'll have to make certain tests, of course, but
I'm confident this is the real thing."

He shook hands solemnly with each of them, as if he
were filled with a sense of this moment's importance.

"I hope," he said, "you'll have no objection to my taking
the piece back with me. Naturally, I'll give you a receipt.
And I'll let you know just as quickly as our findings are
verified. Now I'd better start back."

"Gee, Mr. Clausen," Rick exclaimed, "I'm sorry, but the
ferry only stays here half an hour or so, an' it's the only
one that goes to Hatteras! Now that it's left, you'll have to
stay overnight."

The man from the museum frowned, then shook his
head and broke into a chuckle. "I knew that," he said,

162

"only I was so interested in the relic, I forgot. Well, I've always wanted to see the Outer Banks. Do you suppose they can put me up anywhere here?"

Rick rode with him to the hotel and saw that he got a room. Then he took him home for lunch. Mrs. Landon was a bit flustered at having a guest, but she rose to the occasion and fed him well. Afterward, Clausen suggested that they do some exploring.

Rick guided him down to Springer's Point and the legendary pirate rendezvous. Then they drove up the island as far as they could go by road and crossed the sand on foot to the beach.

Much of the gully had been filled in by the tide in the week since Rick had made his discovery. But there were still a few places where it was deep enough to show unusual beds of shell, old ships' timbers, and bits of rusty iron.

"There have been so many wrecks on this coast," said the Virginian, "I'm really surprised there isn't more to be found. When the German U-boats came in World War I, they sank an average of one ship every day for months. Of course, those were steel vessels—tankers and freighters for the most part—and they went down in deep water, miles from shore."

"I know," said Rick. "I've read about it. Some of 'em were salvaged an' rebuilt afterward. Do you think they'll ever find the *Monitor* an' raise her?"

Clausen looked doubtful. "There've been reports that she was located," he said. "But after nearly a hundred years, lying in three hundred feet of water, it seems pretty unlikely that she could be brought to the surface. I know we'd like to have her. Probably the Smithsonian Institution and others would, too. But at least that piece of her steering wheel is one thing we can keep to remind people of a great little fighting ship."

The museum man left next morning on the northbound

ferry. It was Palm Sunday, and Rick invited him to church, but since a number of cars were waiting for the boat before eleven o'clock, Clausen felt he should stay at the landing and keep his place in line.

"This is a great place," he said. "I've never seen anything just like it, and I want to come back later, when I can spend more time."

*   *   *

On Monday, another visitor arrived from the mainland— a slim, gentle-faced woman with graying hair. Rick didn't see her until after school. He was tossing a baseball with Barney O'Neal when a little red two-seater sports car drove up and stopped.

"Hey," cried Barney. "That's Miss Hamilton! Come on an' say hello to her."

She greeted the bigger boy with a smile that made her look almost beautiful. "How's the young marine biologist?" she asked. "Any birds here for me yet?"

"Sure." Barney laughed. "More of 'em comin' all the toime. Miss Hamilton, this is a friend o' moine—Rick Landon. He's new on the oiland since you were here last spring, but he's interested in birds, too."

Rick shook her firm, small hand and murmured a bashful "Glad to meet you."

"I hear the road's been washed out, up the island," she said. "How about catching me a pony, Barney, and we'll all ride out and see what we can see."

Rick stared at her. Women who rode ponies were something new in his experience. "I know right where Dandelion is," he blurted. "I can have him here in five minutes if you'd like to ride him, Miss Hamilton. Maybe Barney can get you a saddle."

She laughed. "Saddle? Who wants a saddle on Ocracoke? Is Dandelion your horse, Rick? It's a nice name."

164

"Well, ma'am, he belongs to the troop, but I ride him, mostly," Rick explained. "I'll go get him."

He dashed off, his bare feet thudding in the sand. Good as his word, he was back in five minutes with the young palomino. Meanwhile, Barney had rounded up two other ponies. Miss Hamilton got out of the car and stood admiring the golden colt. She was wearing jeans and a flannel shirt that gave her trim figure a boyish look. She patted Dandelion's neck, grasped a handful of his mane, and vaulted easily to his back.

"Okay, pardners!" she called gaily. "Let's hit the trail!"

They had hardly reached the beach when she halted the pony and pointed upward. Flying out across the island to the sea was a big dark bird with a white crest, which she identified as an osprey, or fish hawk. Its broad wings beat steadily as it scanned the water, far below, for fish. While they watched, the osprey dived, plummeting down at terrific speed. There was a splash, a momentary struggle, and the bird rose with a big mullet in its claws.

"Oh—oh," said Miss Hamilton. "Poor old osprey—here comes trouble!"

Following the direction of her pointing finger they saw a dot, high in the sky, that grew rapidly larger as it dropped toward the laboring fish hawk.

"Hey—it's a bald eagle!" Barney exclaimed. "The big bully! He's goin' to steal that fish!"

The osprey saw the larger bird swooping down on it, all fierce yellow eyes and vicious talons. For a moment its wings beat harder in an effort to escape. Then, desperate, it let go of the fish, which the eagle caught in mid-air. As the robber flew off with the loot, the victim of the attack climbed unhappily aloft to resume its search for food.

Miss Hamilton smiled grimly. "That's our national bird," she said. "The eagle's handsome enough, I'll grant, but not a very good symbol of honesty and industry. I don't wonder that naturalists, ever since Audubon, have said we ought to choose a different emblem. The wild turkey, for instance. At least he'd be a true American."

Barney was more practical about it. "I'd go along with you," he said, "but think of all the coins an' monuments an' government seals we'd have to change! Millions an' millions of 'em. Just because the eagle's our national bird it doesn't mean we have to imitate him."

Chapter Eighteen

That ride opened up a whole new world for Rick. In the next two hours Miss Hamilton pointed out birds the boy had never even heard of before.

In addition to the small beach birds Rick had already spotted for himself, she showed them dowitchers, white-rumped sandpipers, and black-bellied plover. A pair of large white terns flying over the surf were identified as Caspian terns. And Miss Hamilton grew really excited when she saw a dark bird with long, graceful wings soaring over the ocean some distance out.

"That's a shearwater!" she cried. "A dusky shearwater, I do believe! Usually they do their migrating out in mid-Atlantic. It's rare for one to come so near shore."

As Barney had told Rick, Miss Hamilton was "folksy" —as much at ease with them as if she had been another boy. She not only rode well, but also talked well. They had gone a long way up the beach when she spied a dense flock of small wading birds ahead of them.

"Let's go slowly and quietly," she said. "Those are knot. Some people call them robin snipe. See the red breasts when they're facing this way? They march like little soldiers in close-order drill, and fly a tight formation when they take off. But the most amazing thing about knot is the distance they travel each year. Right now they're going to their breeding places, way up in northern Greenland, far above the Arctic Circle. That's where they'll nest and hatch their babies. But in August and September they'll be back, heading all the way down to the tip of Patagonia, ten thousand miles south!"

The shy birds saw the riders coming now. They turned in close ranks, facing the wind, waited as if for a starting signal, and went into the air, all of them together, in a split second.

On the way home, the three crossed over and rode along the marshy fringe of the Sound. The black skimmers were there, and Miss Hamilton also pointed out a marsh hawk, sailing far up in the reddening sunset sky. Finally, they saw two graceful white egrets standing like statues in the reeds, and at their approach a great blue heron rose and flapped away to his roosting place in the First Hammock oaks.

Rick had a piece of paper and a stub of pencil in his pocket, and each time they stopped he jotted down the names of the birds. Barney laughed at him, but Miss Hamilton was more understanding.

"It's always a good idea to take notes," she said, "especially when you're learning. Then when you get home, you can remember exactly what you've seen and where."

Rick was grateful for her approval, though what he had had in mind was something different. A week or two earlier, he had been appointed as one of the student editors of the *Ocracoke School News.* It was a lively little paper that came out every month or so, and contained news not only of school affairs but of the village and its happenings. Each issue was made up of eight or ten pages, mimeographed and stapled together. Several hundred copies were run off and sent not only to townspeople but to many subscribers on the mainland. Former islanders and summer visitors liked to read the news of Ocracoke. And to local boys on

168

military service in camps and ships around the world, it brought a friendly link with home.

Rick liked to write. Mrs. Richards had praised some of the compositions he turned in for English class, and it was at her suggestion that he had tried out for student editor. Now he represented the ninth grade on the *School News*.

After supper that evening, he sat down at the table with paper and pencils and started his article. The headline he chose, after much frowning and erasing, was "FAMOUS AUTHORESS REVISITS OCRACOKE." Once he had that down, the rest came more easily.

"This week," he wrote, "Miss Rebecca Hamilton came back to Ocracoke, driving her red Austin-Healey sports car. When interviewed by your reporter, she said the spring migration of sea birds was the reason for her visit. One of the first things Miss Hamilton did was to ask for a pony so she could ride up the island. She rode the good-looking palomino named Dandelion and was accompanied by two members of Troop 290."

He went on to tell where they had gone and listed the birds they had seen that afternoon, putting in some of the lady naturalist's comments. At the end he wrote:

"Miss Hamilton has written a number of books, including the best-selling one, *Between the Dunes and the Sea,* which tells about the Outer Banks. She writes about the ocean and the fish and animals that live in it, besides the birds. She has been called one of America's foremost marine biologists, but, to the folks on Ocracoke, she is best known as a good friend."

It was late when he finished, and he had filled more than three closely written pages. Too long, he thought. The usual contribution from one of the grade editors was only about a paragraph. Still, if they didn't want it, perhaps he could use it as a theme for English.

He took the story to school with him next morning and kept it in his desk until the noon recess. Mrs. Randall acted as faculty adviser to the editorial board. She kept a motherly eye on the contributions, correcting occasional lapses in grammar, and sometimes she herself wrote accounts of major events, such as pony-pennings, hurricanes, or rescues at sea.

Rick waited till most of the other pupils had gone home to dinner. Then he went to Mrs. Randall's room. She was at her desk, eating an apple and correcting papers, when she heard his footstep.

"Well, Rick Landon!" she said. "Not hungry today?"

"No, ma'am—not very. Anyhow, I wanted to ask you something. It's about a piece I wrote for the paper."

She took the sheets of manuscript and whistled. "There seems to be a lot of it. Must have been big happenings in the ninth grade. Let's see what you have to say."

As she read, she nibbled at the apple absent-mindedly. Once or twice she nodded or smiled. At least he could see she was really reading what he had written, not just skimming it.

When she looked up, there was an odd expression in her eyes. It was as if she were seeing him for the first time.

"It *is* pretty long," she said after a moment. "Typed, it would fill more than a page. But we can cut a little here and there. It's good, Ricky—so good I wish we had room to run every word. Where'd you learn to write like this?"

His relief turned to confusion. "I—I dunno," he said. "I read a lot, an' I guess I try to put words together the way the authors do."

The April issue of the *Ocracoke School News* was to come out the following week, and all the editors were busy with make-up. Judy Ann was taking the typing course, and she was assigned the task of making a stencil for Rick's story. He hadn't seen it since he handed it in to Mrs. Ran-

170

dall. Judy Ann came to him in the yard one morning at recess, her eyes round with excitement.

"Golly, Rick," she said, "that's a wonderful article you wrote about Miss Hamilton. I bet that's the first time a freshman ever got a whole page in the paper. I've just finished the stencil. Want to see it?"

He handled the sheet with care, though in his eagerness his fingers seemed clumsy. There it was—his headline and almost all his copy! But what pleased him most was the by-line, right at the top—"By Rick Landon (9th)."

With some trepidation he waited for the paper to be published. Only two or three of the other editors knew about his contribution, for he had made Judy Ann promise not to tell anyone. The big day came at last. By noon, the stapling had been finished, and Rick grabbed a copy and hurried home.

His mother was putting chowder and bread and butter on the table when he came whistling in the back door.

"Oh," she said, "I see you've got the *School News*. I'll have to read it when I get time. Anything in it by the ninth-grade editor?"

"Sure," he replied, trying to sound casual. "You'll find it on page three."

He applied himself to his lunch, but didn't eat very much. His eyes were on his mother. Finally, Joey spoke up with his mouth half full of pie.

"You better read it, Ma," he said. "Rick won't eat till you do. All the kids are talkin' about what a smart writer you got fer a son."

Puzzled, she looked from one boy to the other, then picked up the yellow paper and opened it to page three. "Must be somewhere else," she said. "This is all one long article about visitors to the island."

"No," Rick told her. "That's it. Look under the headline."

Mrs. Landon's mouth dropped open. "For heaven's sake!" She gasped. " 'By Rick Landon'!"

She began to read it aloud, and the words fell pleasantly on Rick's ears. He was prouder at that moment than he had been since the Fourth of July and the pony-penning.

That evening Miss Hamilton's little red roadster pulled up in front of the house. She saw Rick at the front door and waved to him.

"I'm leaving tomorrow," she called. "But I couldn't go till I'd seen you. I read the *Ocracoke School News* today—Mrs. Randall gave me a copy. That was a fine story you wrote about the birds we saw, and what you said about me was one of the nicest compliments I ever had. Good-by and good luck, Rick. Someday I know you'll be a real author!"

He was at the gate by that time and went out to the car, his cheeks flushed with embarrassment. "Gee, Miss Hamilton," he said, "maybe I will, if you think so. I sure hope you'll come back soon. I'll keep Dandelion all slicked up for you to ride."

Smiling, she shook his hand. "I'll come back," she said. "That's a promise. And keep on writing!"

The engine purred and she was off down the road. Rick stood there looking after her, a new ambition stirring in his soul. Miss Hamilton believed in him, and he wasn't going to disappoint her if he could help it.

*   *   *

The full tide of spring had come to Ocracoke now. The yards blazed with color, for the oleander was in bloom and there were tulips and daffodils in many gardens. Hundreds of small birds sang and flitted through the trees as the warblers migrated northward. There were so many different kinds that Rick was lucky to identify half of them, even with the help of the Randalls' bird books.

172

Almost a thousand dollars had been raised for the pony-fencing fund, thanks to generous gifts from on and off the island. Posts were already being set and wire strung, though it would be some time before the whole range was enclosed.

Meanwhile, the boys played ball, rode horseback, and, as soon as the water warmed up, went swimming in the Sound. This was the time of year when boats were hauled out, caulked, and painted. Rick made a few dollars helping with these jobs. He also got to know some of the fishermen, and when Eph Garrish invited him for a trip in his shrimp boat, the *Ellie May*, he was more than happy to accept.

The shrimper was thirty-eight feet long, powered by a rugged diesel engine, and carried two men besides the skipper. They made an early start and cruised northeastward for three hours. There wasn't much for Rick to do until they reached the fishing grounds, up in the middle of Pamlico Sound, halfway to Oregon Inlet. There the small try net was let down, and the boat pulled it slowly along the bottom for a mile or two. When it was brought to the surface, there were a dozen or more shrimp in the meshes.

"Looks fair to middlin'," said the captain. "Git the big net over."

The large dragnet was worked from a boom on the mast, since it was too heavy to be handled manually. It was fitted with a pair of big wing boards, or vanes, that held the mouth open as it was dragged along the bottom. Rick helped the others at the winch, and they soon had the net in action. Eph Garrish opened the throttle a little. They cruised up and down the Sound for an hour and a half, checking with the try net every few minutes. Sometimes it came up empty, but more often it held a few shrimp.

Finally, at the end of ninety minutes, the winch was started again, and the big net came slowly upward with water pouring out of it on the afterdeck. The crew cheered, for as it rose higher, they could see it bulging with the squirming silvery catch. There were shrimp in the net, but there were many other things besides. The skipper put on oilskins and rubber gloves before sorting the haul, and his men did the same.

"Rick," Garrish called. "Go fetch some o' them boxes with the oice in 'em."

By the time he had hauled three boxes aft, the crew were heaving unwanted fish, crabs, and seaweed overboard. Gulls by the score had gathered for the feast, screaming and diving around the boat. The deck was slippery with scales and slime, but the pile of shrimp mounted higher and higher. One of the men brought a big shovel and scooped them into the boxes on top of the crushed ice.

"Pretty good haul," said Garrish with satisfaction. "Oi'd say eighty pound from that one drag. Put her over again, boys."

By three o'clock that afternoon they had made two more sweeps with the net and filled eight boxes—all they had brought with them. The skipper was in a good mood. "Take the wheel, Amos," he called. "Oi'll go make us some coffee to drink on the way home."

When the pot was bubbling and their tin cups were full of the black, steamy brew, he leaned against the side of the little pilothouse and told Rick about shrimping in the old days.

"Used to come in with twelve or fifteen boxes loaded every trip," he said. "Oi've took in a thousand dollars cash in a week's shrimpin'. Here lately, though, somethin' seems to have mommicked 'em. Most o' last season we didn't make enough to keep us in terbaccer. These here are big shrimp—first run o' the summer jumbos, looks loike. Could be they're comin' back."

174

Chapter Nineteen

For a week or two after Mr. Clausen's visit to the island, Rick often wondered when some word would come from the museum. He thought there would be a lot of satisfaction in knowing the old wheel was genuine—that he had actually found and handled an important bit of American history.

In the meantime, he kept busy, both outdoors and in school. Each evening, when his homework was out of the way, he did a little writing. Miss Hamilton had given him a real incentive to improve in that field. Some of the things he wrote were short stories—imaginative yarns about pirate days on the island. But the ones he liked best were true accounts of things he had seen for himself. He described the annual pony roundup, for instance. Then he tried to create a vivid word-picture of the autumn hurricane, a rescue by the Coast Guard, or the day's work aboard a shrimp boat. It was all good practice, and he knew he was doing better, week by week.

With all these things to occupy him, he gradually stopped worrying about the *Monitor*'s steering wheel and hardly thought of it as April slipped by. His birthday was coming soon, and he would be fifteen. Sometimes he tried to remember how he had felt about his last birthday. Those recollections of Brooklyn made him a little ashamed of himself now. What an ungrateful brat he had been!

There was still no television set in their home, but who needed one? If there was a special show he wanted to see, he could always go to Jed's or Coley's house. But the Westerns he had once pined for now seemed tame, compared to the real-life thrill of galloping over the dunes with a horse like Dandelion under him.

Some of the older boys in the Scout troop were ambitious to own cars. There were plenty of broken-down or abandoned jalopies on the island, and they spent most of their spare time tinkering with old engines, trying to make them run. Some day Rick supposed he would be bitten by the same bug, but for the present he was content. For the first time in his life, it wasn't easy to think of anything he wanted as a birthday gift.

The first week in May, he came home from school one afternoon and remembered that his mother had asked him to spade a garden in the back yard. She wasn't there, for she worked in the store several hours a day. Rick laid out a plot about twenty by forty feet, spat on his hands, and started digging up the sandy loam. He didn't know just where Joey had gone. Anyhow, the younger boy would have been little help with the job. An hour went by, and he was just turning over the final spadeful of earth when he heard the thud of bare feet racing up the road.

"Hey!" Joey panted as he sped through the gate. "A letter—for you! It's postmarked Newport News!"

Rick wiped his hands on his dungarees and took the envelope. There was the address, sure enough—"Master Richard Landon, Ocracoke, N.C."

Eagerly he ripped it open and took out the letter. It was on the letterhead of the Mariners' Museum.

"Dear Rick," it began. "You have doubtless wondered

176

what has happened in regard to the section of steering wheel you discovered. For nearly a month it has been at a research laboratory in Washington, where exhaustive tests were made. Now we have the piece back, together with the report. Chemical tests, X rays, and careful microscopic study all prove beyond doubt that the wheel came from the U.S. warship *Monitor*. Congratulations!

"We have a small fund available for remunerating those who turn over valuable discoveries to the museum. Enclosed is our check for $100.00. I'm sure you will find good use for it."

It was signed, "Sincerely, H. M. Clausen, Associate Curator."

Rick stooped and picked up the green slip of paper that had fallen on the ground. "Gosh!" He gulped. "Look at that! They sent me a hundred dollars!"

Joey was too much impressed to say anything at first, but his eyes widened as he stared at the check. Finally he managed to speak in a whisper. "Whatcha goin' to do with it?" he asked.

Rick laughed. "Do with it? See if Ma needs it, I guess, or put it in the savings account. First, though, I've got to tell Mr. Randall the news."

He found the school principal still working at his desk. Mr. Randall read the letter quickly, then jumped up and slapped him on the back.

"You've a right to be proud, Rick!" he exclaimed. "Not just about the money, I mean, but the fact that thousands of people—visitors to the museum from all over the country—will see that piece of wheel. They'll read the inscription under it, too, and see that it was found on the beach at Ocracoke by a fellow named Rick Landon!"

"Gee," said Rick breathlessly, "that's right. Maybe someday I can go up there an' see it myself."

He was waiting at home when his mother came in. She looked tired, but the letter and the check cheered her up at once.

"Of course," she said, "there are a lot of ways we could get rid of a hundred dollars. New clothes, or having electricity put in—or a fine birthday present for you. But we're doing well enough. What I'd do in your place is send the money right to Postal Savings. If you're going to be a writer, you'll need money for college some day."

Not many people in school or in the village knew about the *Monitor* wheel. Rick and the principal had said nothing about it, and Joey had kept the secret, though he was itching to tell. Now it came out. The next issue of the *Ocracoke School News* carried the whole story, written by Mr. Randall, and created a considerable stir on the island. People stopped Rick on the street to congratulate him.

There was only one dissenting voice. Windy Jenkins, who spent most of his time envying other people, dropped the remark that some folks would do almost anything to get their names in print. That was in the schoolyard, just after Rick had tagged him out at second in a choose-up-sides ball game. Rick overheard the words and went up to Jenkins at once.

"Meaning me?" he asked without raising his voice.

Windy backed away. "Naw," he replied hastily. "I mean everybody in this cheap burg. Won't have to take it much longer, though. We're movin' up to Manteo, where Paw can make some decent money with fishin' parties."

"Good," said Rick. "I'm sure you'll find more o' your kind o' people up there—real sports."

* * *

A mockingbird in the live oak just outside his window woke Rick on the morning of his birthday. He stretched

178

luxuriously and grinned at the play of sunlight on the sill. It was going to be a good day, whether he got any presents or not.

Joey was already up. Rick could hear him talking in a low, excited voice downstairs. A fragrance of coffee and of muffins that were just being taken out of the oven came up to him. He dressed fast.

At his place at the kitchen table was a big, awkward package, done up with a length of left-over Christmas ribbon.

"Happy birthday, son!" his mother said. "Yes, it's for you, but don't open it till after we've said grace. I'm just about to put things on the table."

He waited with what patience he could muster. When at last he began to untie the ribbon, Joey watched him with shining eyes.

"It's from Ma an' me," the little boy crowed. "I made some money runnin' errands. 'Tisn't new, but it's a good 'un."

Inside the wrapping, Rick found a typewriter! Some of the paint had been scratched and worn, but he could see it was a good make and in working condition. At first he was unable to say anything. Then he got up and went around the table to hug his mother and Joey.

"I guess," he told them shakily, "I really do have to be a writer now!"

Typing wasn't among Rick's subjects at school, but he got Judy Ann to help him learn the touch system. Two or three evenings a week, she stopped by after school and put him through his practice exercises. He found it a bit hard to concentrate on the keys with her pretty face and dark fluffy hair so near his shoulder. But she was serious about it.

"Stop looking at me, Rick Landon," she told him tartly.

"You're going to learn to type whether you like it or not, and the only reason I'm here is to see that you do. Now—start over."

He laughed. "It's a good thing you plan to be a schoolteacher," he said, teasing her. "You'll make 'em toe the mark. Won't be any fooling in your classes."

But he worked hard at it after she left. One of his traits was a dogged persistence that made him finish what he started.

As May went by, the tempo of affairs quickened in the village. Party-boat fishermen painted their craft and laid in tackle. Two small motels were finished and made ready for visitors.The number of cars that came in by ferry increased, and state employees with big highway machines were working hard to rebuild the island road.

At school, the senior class was both sobered and excited by the prospect of graduation, now looming so near. There was to be a Senior Prom this year—not just a square dance, but the regular ballroom kind, with a five-piece orchestra all the way from Elizabeth City. All the high school pupils pitched in to help decorate the recreation hall with bright crepe-paper streamers.

There were only nine in the graduating class, five boys and four girls. Sally Dennis and two of the other girls were going on to college on the mainland. Among the boys, only Barney O'Neal had college in mind. The rest planned to go directly into military service—three of them choosing Coast Guard enlistments.

Barney confided to Rick that he was still worried about being accepted. He had studied hard in his science courses and put in many hours of overtime to complete his laboratory work. But the requirements were stiff. It wasn't until June, a few days before school ended, that he got word from a northern university saying his application was approved. All his friends had been pulling for him, and the jubilation was general.

As he looked ahead, Rick wondered how he would be feeling on the eve of his own graduation. But three years was a long time. He needn't start worrying about college yet. He dressed in his best and took Judy Ann to the prom. Jitterbugging wasn't too hard, he found, if you had rhythm and lively feet and a partner as responsive as his. For a steady diet, though, they both decided they liked square dancing best.

Because this was a special occasion, the dance lasted much later than usual. It was nearly two when Rick walked Judy Ann home through the moonlight. There was a scent of roses and jasmine in the soft air, and when they said good night, he kissed her for the first time. He wasn't sure afterward whether he had been walking or flying on his way home.

*   *   *

As soon as school was over, the Scout troop began making preparations for the Fourth of July celebration. They had been too busy for much riding during the past month, and the ponies had been left to themselves.

"They'll be plenty woild an' spooky, come toime fer the roundup," Jed Rowan remarked. "But after what happened in the hurricane, there won't be so many of 'em to bring in, poor little fellers."

"I'm anxious to see how Dandelion's making out," said Rick. "He's been up-island ever since the new grass came in. Probably fat an' sassy by now. If we're going to ride in the parade, we'd better go up there soon an' cut the Scout ponies out o' the herd."

They talked it over with Captain Howard, and the next day he took Rick, Jed, and Coley in his jeep to collect enough mounts for the troop. The state highway crews were working about halfway up the island, and the roar and rumble of their heavy equipment could be heard for miles.

"Won't be any ponies this side o' Quork Hammock, with all that racket," the captain grumbled.

He was right. There wasn't so much as a track to be seen until they had left the road builders far behind. Then, crossing the Tar Hole Plains, they sighted a bunch of the little horses ahead, near Styrons' Hills.

"Hey!" said Coley. "What's goin' on up there? Looks to be a foight o' some kind!"

Rick's heart beat faster. He had caught a glimpse of a tawny-colored body rearing high in the air, and a pale mane and tail streaming in the wind. "It's the palomino," he gasped. "He's fighting with the brown stallion!"

Captain Howard drove ahead faster through the sand. "Hate to see that colt get hurt," was all he said.

No attention was paid by the herd to the approaching car. The mares, foals, and geldings stood in a nervous huddle, watching the battle seesaw back and forth. Dandelion had grown a little that year, but he was still outweighed by the brown horse. He had to make up in speed and spirit what he lacked in poundage.

The two stallions circled each other, squealing, rearing, biting, and striking out with their forefeet. Once Rick thought his favorite was beaten, for the brown stallion got a vicious grip with his teeth high on the back of the colt's neck. But Dandelion wrenched free and instantly attacked again. With a lightning stroke of his hoof, he caught his adversary in the shoulder. The bigger horse staggered back, wavered a second, then broke and ran. With a fierce neigh the palomino raced after him, nipping at his quarters, until he disappeared in the woods.

"Well, well!" The captain chuckled. "I reckon the herd has got a brand-new leader."

182

Dandelion came prancing back to the bunched ponies, his eyes flashing proudly, his head and tail high.

"Whew!" Jed whistled, wiping his brow. "Oi don't know's anybody kin roide him now, Rick. He's settin' in the catbird seat an' thinks he's ten foot tall!"

Rick didn't answer. He had climbed out of the jeep and was walking slowly toward the herd. The idea of being afraid of the victorious stallion never crossed his mind. All he saw was the blood clotting on that wound behind the ears.

"Dandelion," he called gently. "You're hurt, boy. Come here an' let me fix it. Come on. See? I've got an apple for you."

The palomino snorted once. Then, to the amazement of the other Scouts, he started walking toward the boy. He came slowly, ears pricked forward and head stretched out. There was nothing menacing in his approach, but they all heaved a sigh of relief when they saw him take the proffered apple and submit to his friend's gentle patting. A moment later Rick had swung up to his back.

"Okay, you guys," he called gaily. "Come an' get your ponies!"

Chapter Twenty

The damage to Dandelion's neck turned out to be not too serious, and though he had other bruises, they healed quickly. Rick bathed the open cuts with a weak carbolic solution and kept the colt securely tied in the back yard, where he could nurse and groom him. There were fifteen or twenty other ponies in the village, brought down for the penning and the parade, so the palomino didn't object too much to being away from the main herd.

On the morning of the Fourth, Rick gave Dandelion's coat a final brushing, put a bridle on him, and rode out to join the rest of the troop. The boy had had his hair cut at Jackson's one-chair barbershop and was wearing his freshly pressed Scout outfit.

It was a perfect July day, sunny but with a cool south breeze. They found the herd at the upper end of the island and brought them down without too much trouble. Once or twice Dandelion laid his ears back at sight of the brown stallion, but Rick kept him firmly in check.

There were several new foals running beside their mothers. At least two were tawny yellow in color, and their fuzzy little manes and tails were a pale silver. Rick grinned to himself when he saw them. "Going to be more palominos around here, now that you're the boss," he told his mount.

It was a little before noon when the ponies were herded

across the Park Service area and into the main street, lined with the usual throng of spectators. Amid clouds of dust, they went thundering past the post office, rounded the bend, and were driven through the open gate of the corral.

As soon as the bars were closed behind the ponies, everybody started home to dinner. Rick rode by a roundabout route, for he hoped to get a look at Judy Ann's parade costume. She had been picked as one of the princesses on the Miss Ocracoke float. As he passed the ice plant, he saw that the ferry had just come in from Hatteras, and the first cars were rolling down the ramp.

One of them was a plain-looking little Ford coupé, four or five years old. It had New York license plates, not too uncommon among summer visitors, and he saw a man and woman inside. As he rode on toward the Fulchers' house, something kept bothering him. Was he wrong or did that couple remind him of two people he ought to know? He started to turn the pony back, but by then the car had driven away.

Judy Ann wasn't at home. She had gone to another girl's house to get ready for the parade, Coley informed him. Disappointed, he rode home, rubbed the pony down to remove the sweat and dust of the morning's work, and went in to dinner.

"Guess who stopped by here a few minutes ago," his mother greeted him. "No, that's not fair—you'd never guess in the world. It's that young policeman that arrested you once—Officer McClure. And he's got his bride with him. Remember Miss Vronsky? Well, they got married last week, and they're down here on their honeymoon!"

The news fairly knocked Rick off his feet. "Honest?" He gasped. "I saw a car—say, tell me, were they in a black Ford coupé? No wonder I thought I knew 'em! Where are they staying?"

186

"Silver Lake Inn," she told him. "So they'll be right handy for the parade an' branding the colts. Both of 'em asked about you, Rick. They weren't sure, but they thought they saw you, down by the landing."

The floats were already moving into position in the Coast Guard parking lot when Rick got there. Since the parade wouldn't be starting for another ten minutes, he went over to admire Miss Ocracoke and her attendant princesses. Judy Ann was wearing a dress of fluffy yellow tulle that set off her dark curls and made her look, Rick thought, like a somewhat impish angel. She held on to her perch with one hand, leaned down, and planted a kiss on Dandelion's velvet nose. The band started tootling at that moment, and the colt reared and pirouetted while Judy Ann pulled back in haste.

Rick laughed. "See you later," he told her. "There's some folks down here that I want you to meet."

He rode over to the front rank of the assembled troop. He and Jed had been elected to the color guard this year, and they lined up on either side of Coley Fulcher, who carried the flag.

Captain Howard, on his own big gray horse, was acting as Grand Marshal. "All set, back there?" he shouted above the noise. "All right, then, let's have a good lively march tune!"

The cornets blared out the opening notes, the trombones joined in, and the tuba and drums took up the bass. Sitting proudly erect on their ponies, the color guard and the rest of the troop rode out to the head of the street. And behind them, the engines in the float trucks coughed and rumbled. Ahead stood two solid lines of waving, cheering people.

The ponies behaved well. Once or twice Dandelion broke into a little dance step, as if he remembered the Labor Day Jamboree, but Rick steadied him with an easy rein.

Not until they had made the turn and were riding toward

the corral did the boy see his old friends. They were standing there beside the fence—the tall, square-jawed Irishman,
now in civilian slacks and sport shirt, and his bride. Little
Mrs. McClure was smiling and waving. She looked prettier
than the Miss Vronsky Rick remembered. Perhaps getting
married had done that.

When the parade broke up, the other Scouts tackled the
job of cutting out and branding the foals. Rick excused
himself. He could hardly wait to reach the Brooklyn couple.

As soon as he swung off the palomino and pushed his
way toward them, however, he found himself strangely
tongue-tied. It was his former teacher who broke the ice.

"Rick!" she cried and threw her arms around him. "We
hardly knew you—you look so big and brown! Shake hands
with another old friend of yours—my husband."

McClure gave him an iron grip. "Sure and it's fine to see ye, lad." He chuckled. "An' that's a lovely little horse ye were ridin'. Somebody told us ye broke him yerself!"

"I was stupid to try it," Rick mumbled, red-faced, "but I had some luck. Tell me—how'd you get way down here?"

"We came to see you," said Mrs. McClure with a laugh. "You see, Rick, if it hadn't been for the trouble you got into, Mike and I would never have met. So, when we'd set the wedding date and were wondering where to go on our honeymoon, we both thought of it at once—Ocracoke!"

"Well," said Rick, "I think it's wonderful, an' I sure am glad you're here. How about coming to the square dance tonight? There's a lot of nice people here I want you to know. So be sure to be there at eight o'clock."

He saw them that night as soon as he and Judy Ann entered the hall. The girl and Mrs. McClure took to each other at once. By the end of the first figure, Judy Ann had persuaded them to join a set. The big policeman soon unlimbered, and before it was over, he was swinging his partner with as much dash as anybody on the floor.

Rick introduced the couple to Barney, Jed, and Coley and their girls, then brought the Randalls over to meet them.

"So you're the Miss Vronsky I've heard about." Carolyn Randall smiled. "This boy Rick has spoken of you more than once. Whatever else he got out of his school in the city, you did something for him that hasn't worn off."

Embarrassed, Rick turned away, but not before he heard the principal's wife start to talk about his writing. He left the four married people together and took Judy Ann out on the floor for the next dance.

At the end of the evening, the McClures thanked him for all the fun they had had. Miss Vronsky—he still thought of her by that name—asked if he could take a ride with them in their car in the morning.

"We're eager to see the island and we need a guide," she explained.

"You bet," he said, delighted. "I'd like it a lot." Shortly after breakfast the Ford appeared and Rick climbed in beside his one-time teacher. They rode down to the lighthouse and Springer's Point, then headed out the state road as far as it was usable. Crossing the flats on foot, they came to the beach. The tide was out, and the sand was alive with gulls, terns, and sandpipers.

Rick told the visitors about his interest in birds and about Miss Hamilton. "You ought to meet her," he said. "She's a wonderful person."

"I'm sure she is," Mrs. McClure answered. "I've read some of her books and loved them. Tell me, Rick, are you serious about wanting to write?"

He thought a minute before he spoke. "Yes," he said. "I guess it's what I want more than anything. I'll probably have to have another job, though, and write on the side. I'd like to go to college if I can save up enough."

He told them about some of the ways Ocracoke boys had of earning a little money.

"Sounds to me like a pretty good kind of a life," Officer McClure put in. "I'm beginnin' to see how a place like this gets along without any police, but they tell me there's no doctors, either. What happens if somebody gets sick or a woman's havin' a baby?"

"Well," said Rick, "we've got Miss Craig, the village nurse. She takes care o' the babies, an' things like colds an' croup an' stomach-aches. But if anybody's hurt, or gets real sick, the Coast Guard flies 'em to a hospital." And he described the gunning accident of the past fall.

"We don't even have a reg'lar fire department," he added. "But they have some equipment at the Coast Guard station, an' they're used to handling 'most any kind of emergencies."

Mrs. McClure smiled. "You're a pretty loyal Ocracoker,

aren't you, Rick?" she said. "Like it better than Brooklyn?"

He looked at her in surprise, but he saw that the question was serious.

"A lot better," he said. "I'd never have amounted to much if I'd stayed there. A guy wants to *be* somebody. He thinks he has to belong. I suppose I might have found a boys' club, or a Y.M.C.A., or even a Scout troop to belong to. But all the big shots in school laughed at that sort o' stuff. You know—guys like Rocky, an' Big Jake, an' Tony Lambretta. So when they took Ziggy an' me into the Owls, we thought we'd done something big.

"Right at first I didn't go for living on the island much, but I got over that in a hurry. The kids here are a swell bunch, an' the grownups, too. You ought to see our school!"

Mike McClure looked at his bride and grinned. "Ye got yer answer, me girl," he said. "An' a good one, too. The lad's right. I'd not mind livin' here meself. It's a real shame they're not in need of a cop, but we can come down again on vacations."

*　　*　　*

They all went for a swim that afternoon, and in the evening the young honeymooners were invited to the Randalls'. Left to himself, Rick sat on the back steps and drank in the sea-flavored freshness of the summer night. That morning had been the first time he had ever put his feeling about Ocracoke into words, and he knew what he had said was true. Here he *really* belonged.

There came a sound of restless movement and a soft whinny from the rear of the yard. He remembered then that Dandelion was still tied up. From the kitchen he brought an apple and went out to take the halter off the palomino. He waited till the last bit of fruit was eaten, then gave the pony a gentle slap on the flank.

"Sorry, boy," he said. "I forgot you might be lonesome. I won't be needing you to ride for a while, so go on an' find the rest o' the bunch."

Dandelion understood. He nuzzled Rick's hand briefly, then pricked up his ears, jumped nimbly over the picket fence, and cantered away up the road, heading for the wild salt-grass pastures where he, too, belonged.